MY MOTHER REBELS

JACKIE GRANGER

ISBN: 1500763373
ISBN 13: 9781500763374
Library of Congress Control Number: 2014914894

CreateSpace Independent Publishing Platform
North Charleston, South Carolina

PROLOGUE

I am constantly amazed at how a seemingly random event happening in one place can affect the outcome of another random event happening in a different place. Actually, I started to pay attention to these types of correlations when I was a teenager. That's when my mother told us the story of what happened to my younger sister, Jane, when she was two years old.

My older brother, Bernie, and I were already in school. My father was at work, so it was just my mother and Jane at home. There were no cell phones back then. The 911 emergency phone number hadn't been invented yet. If you needed help, you had look up the number in the phone book, then determine who was the specific responder in your area before you could even make a call.

One day my sister had a grand-mal seizure. Rather than wasting time locating the phone book, deciding which emergency responder to call – the county Sheriff's Department or the

Town Police Department – then actually making the call, the first thing my mother did was run outside to see if there were any neighbors in their yards who could help. And, there, just two driveways down from our house, was a deputy sheriff sitting in a squad car. The deputy had made a wrong turn and was in the process of turning around.

You see if my mother hadn't run out of the house first, she would have missed the deputy who was a mere two driveways away. And by the same token, if the deputy hadn't taken the wrong street causing him to turn around in that driveway, he would have missed my mother who desperately needed his help.

Since then, I have seen these types of random acts happen over and over again. To prove my point, I want to tell you about one that started five months ago when my brother convinced Jane and me that our seventy-one year old, widowed mother had to sell her large house and move into a senior complex. Not only that, he also convinced the two of us to go with him when he confronted her.

To be honest, the three of us should have known better. We should have seen it coming. Our mother did not appreciate us trying to make decisions for her. To put it in the vernacular of my teenage children, "When you guys ganged up on Grandma, she got pissed off".

And, that is the first random event in this scenario.

CHAPTER 1

She pressed speed dial and waited for her friend to answer. "Pauline? This is Katherine. I'm going to take you to lunch. I'll be over in 30 minutes."

She listened to her friend's answer. "Well, screw the gentle aerobics class, Pauline. I need you. Get dressed and be in the lobby in 30 minutes."

After she hung up, she dialed another number.

"Arthur? It's Katherine. I need to see you today. Are you free this afternoon around two-thirty?

"No, no. I'm fine, but I do need to see you."

"Good. I'll be at your office at two-thirty."

The women sat at a table for two in the small café. Pauline took a sip of coffee and looked over at Katherine.

"So, are you going to tell me what this is all about? You know, I could be having wicked thoughts about my eye-candy, aerobics instructor right now."

With elbows on the table Katherine leaned forward and stared intently at her friend. "Pauline, you and I are going to go backpacking through Europe. Get everything ready. I'll make all the arrangements. We'll leave as soon as we can."

"What?" Pauline asked incredulously with her coffee mug half way to her lips. She slowly placed the mug on the table.

"You're serious, aren't you?" She reached over and laid her hand on Katherine's arm. "Okay, my friend. What's going on?"

They had been friends for over fifty-five years and could practically finish each other's sentences. Neither of them needed to articulate for the other to know when something was wrong.

Katherine swallowed and blinked away the tears. After a moment she got herself under control.

"I love my children dearly, but sometimes they drive me nuts. They came to see me this morning. They want me to sell my house and move into a senior complex. What really hurts, Pauline? I mean beside the fact they think I'm old," she interjected. "They think they have the right to barge into my life and make decisions for me. I'm just furious."

She looked down at her friend's hand on her arm. "After they left, I thought about my life. Do you know John and I never did anything spontaneous? We never had a spur-of-the-moment adventure. Oh, sure, we traveled, but it was always planned down to the last detail. We never left room for exploring on our own."

Katherine paused and brushed some crumbs on the tablecloth. She looked up at Pauline and spoke softly. "Maybe I will go into that senior complex. But not yet," she added with emphasis. "I want a chance to have the adventures I never had. Come with me. We'll go to Europe with no set itinerary."

Pauline smiled and slowly shook her head. "Oh, Katherine. Ever since we were teenagers, you've always talked me into doing crazy things. But we're not two kids anymore. We're 71 years old. Good grief, I have to take 10 different pills a day. Just my pills alone would fill a suitcase."

Katherine leaned forward and looked her friend directly in the eye. "You know how men tell each other to get balls? Well, woman-to-woman, get a uterus, Pauline."

Pauline chuckled. "I had a hysterectomy 15 years ago. You know that."

"Well, get it back," Katherine said forcefully. "Ah, come on. How many more chances will we have? Right now, we're in relatively good health. So, we walk a little slower. Big deal."

Katherine spoke without malice. This was her friend since high school. "You know as well as I do, it was your children who made you go into that senior condo." Pauline sucked in air and jerked back slightly at the truthfulness of Katherine's words. She stared back across the table with a look of sadness on her face.

Katherine reached across the table and took Pauline's two hands. "Let's do it. Let's have one final, fantastic adventure. This may be our last chance, kiddo."

Pauline looked out the windows of the cafe. She became lost in thought. Then with her lips together a smile appeared. "Oh, why the heck not? But, no back-packs," she added. "Sling one of those babies on our backs and we'll tip over backwards and end up on the floor before we even get out the front door."

The two childhood friends began to plan what they were going to do on their European trip. They giggled just like they did when they were teenagers planning some crazy escapade.

CHAPTER 2

Four months later, Arthur Warner requested the three of us meet him at my mother's house. Arthur had been a friend of my parents and was now my mother's attorney. I picked up Bernie and Jane and we drove together. None of us had a clue about the reason for this summons. Other than telling us to meet him on Saturday afternoon at two, he gave no other hint as to why he wanted us to come to her house. He was waiting at the door when I drove into the driveway.

"Come on in. Bernie, Jane, Priscilla," he acknowledged each of us as we neared the front porch. The three of us looked at each other questioningly. Why wasn't our mother here to meet us?

When we entered the house, we stood with our mouths open. The entire house was bare. All the furnishings were gone! When we came into the living room, there were four folding chairs lined up – three in a row and one off to the side. Oh brother, this doesn't bode well, I thought.

"What the heck is going on?" Bernie asked. "What happened to all my mother's furniture?"

"Has something happened to Mother?" Jane asked on the verge of tears. "Is she all right?"

"What has she done this time?" I asked and rolled my eyes heavenward.

"Sit down. I will explain everything," Arthur said as he pointed to the three chairs. He sat in the chair off to the side and pulled an envelope out of his pocket. He opened it and took out a letter. Holding it up, he said, "Your mother has written you a letter with instructions that I am to read it to you."

> *I suppose I should begin by apologizing to the three of you for taking the easy way out. I'm letting Arthur tell you what I have been up to and where I'm going.*
>
> *Well, as you can see by now, I've sold the house. However, I'm not moving into a senior complex, at least not yet. I decided I'm going to have one last adventure. And, it's a beauty.*
>
> *Pauline and I are going to travel to every country in Europe. We have no set itinerary. We'll go wherever we choose as we try to see them all. And, we have no idea when we'll be back. I'll be sending each of you . . .*

Bernie jumped up and shouted, "What?" then fell back onto his chair.

"Oh, no," I said as I covered my face with my hands.

"Oh, Mother," Jane wailed and reached for a tissue from her purse.

Arthur watched our reactions, then he gave a gentle cough and continued to read Mother's letter.

> *I'll be sending each of you emails periodically to let you know where we are and what we are doing. But, more importantly, through my emails, I want each of you to share these adventures with me. (Arthur, this might be a good time to get the brandy out.)*

The three of us flew out of our chairs like space shuttles taking off from launch pads and began talking at once.

"What?" Jane wailed.

"She can't do this to us," I shouted.

"This is horrible," Bernie chimed in. "I'm going to take steps to freeze her accounts so she can't get at the money. She can't just throw it away on something as stupid as this!"

"Afraid not, Bernie," Arthur said with a slight grin on his face. "The accounts are all in her name. You have no legal standing."

"Then I'm going to have her declared incompetent, because taking off for God-knows-where at her age surely proves she's off her rocker," Bernie shouted.

"Afraid not on that one either." Arthur really seemed to be enjoying this. "In order for a court to declare incompetency, they would have to interview her, but she's no longer in the country."

"Well, where is she?" Bernie asked stunned.

Arthur looked at his watch. "Right now your mother and Pauline should be somewhere in the middle of the English countryside having a pint of ale with the locals. By the way, your mother would like you all to join me in a toast to her adventure." Arthur reached into his briefcase and pulled out a bottle of brandy.

"Forget it, Arthur," Bernie said in disgust. "There is absolutely nothing to celebrate. In fact, I'm leaving right now." He slammed the door on his way out.

"How could she do something like this to us?" Jane said with a tissue to her nose as she also fled.

"Don't look at me. I'm the one driving. I have to take them home," I said on my way to the door.

Arthur remained seated after Katherine's children left. He stared across the empty room and reflected on the past. I have known John and Katherine for over forty-five years, he thought. John and I started out at the same law firm putting in 60 to 80 hours a week. We were young bucks working our way up the law firm ladder.

Arthur had a slight smile on his face as the memories came flooding back. Even though John moved to another firm, we remained friends. Within the obligatory five years, we both made partner in our respective firms. And, now we were big shots. He raised his eyebrows and chuckled.

He spent the next few minutes thinking about all the things they shared over the years – golf on weekends, godparents to each other's children, and later when they had the time and the money, vacations together with their spouses.

Coming out of his reverie, he cocked his head and smiled once again. And, I suppose . . . if I'm truthful with myself . . . I think I had a little crush on you, Katherine. I admired your honesty and vitality. Something was always going on when you were around. People smiled more when you came into their circle. Fortunately, for everyone involved, I was never stupid enough to act on that schoolboy crush . . . but now that we are both widowed, maybe I should.

"Ah well, just the ramblings of an old man," he said out loud and shook his head in amusement.

He leaned down and took a glass out of his brief-case. After he poured the brandy, he raised his glass.

"Bon voyage, Katherine. Have the time of your life, old friend," he whispered in the quietness.

EMAIL
From: Katherine Wilson
To: Bernie Wilson, Priscilla Wilson, Jane Atkins
Subject: Europe

I'm assuming you have all heard from Arthur and know what I have done.

As I promised, I want to keep you in the loop as to what's going on over here. We landed in England last week and are having a grand time. We didn't spend too much time in London. As soon as we could, we rented a car and drove out to the countryside.

And, now we can cross three things off our To Do List – having a pint of ale in an English pub, driving a car on the left side of the road, and having an old man yell out his car window, 'Move your bloomin arse' at us when I had trouble figuring out how to make a right turn from the left hand lane.

Pauline thought the old guy was right out of one of those British comedies we watch on PBS.

Now we're off to Paris. I will write more from there.

Love, Mom

EMAIL
From: Bernie Wilson
To: Katherine Wilson
Subject: Europe

Well, Mom, you have managed to do it again. Just when we thought we had you all figured out, you pulled the rug out from under us and did something unexpected, but so you.

I will say I was quite angry when Arthur told us you left for Europe with Pauline. But, now that I've had time to calm down, I can understand why you did it. We did gang up on you about selling your house, etc. And, to be truthful, if my kids ever pull a stunt like that when I get older, I'll probably act the same way. (Guess who I'll have learned that from?)

Oh, and by the way, using Arthur to tell us what you were up to – wimpy, Mom. Real wimpy.

So, it sounds like you and Pauline are having a good time in England. The thing that really amazed me when Amy and I were there was all the history over the centuries that shaped the country. I told you about renting a metal detector one afternoon and finding an old Roman coin in a field. Good grief. It's thousands of years old! I still carry it with me tucked in my wallet.

Have fun and keep the emails coming.

P.S. I'm making a list of senior living places for you to visit when you finally come home.

Love, Bernie

EMAIL
To: Dennie Maddich, Rosie Edwards
From: Pauline Maddich
Subject: Europe

This is to let you know that I'm in Europe with Katherine. I know it's a big surprise for you to digest. Sorry I didn't tell you before I left, but I felt it would be easier this way – a sort of after the fact.

Why did we do it? Well, we felt at our age, this may be our last hurrah . . . or maybe not. I will be sending you emails periodically to let you know where we are. I would like to be able to share these things with you as we go along.

We hit England at just the right time of year. The flowers are blooming and it is just beautiful here. We're spending most of our time in the countryside rather than in London. The people we've met are so kind.

I love you both. Kiss the grandchildren for me. Love, Mom

EMAIL
To: Pauline Maddich
From: Dennis Maddich
Subject: Idiotic Stunt

Well, I certainly hope you're enjoying yourself in Europe. You're too old to be pulling sophomoric stunts like this. And, then going off without telling us. Sending an email from England informing us of your whereabouts is about the dumbest thing you could do.

What do we do if something happens to you? Will you expect us to fly over there to help you?

You need to come home. If you want adventure, go shopping at the Mall like all the other people your age.

I'm sorry Mom, but I just can't share this adventure with you.

Dennis

EMAIL
To: Pauline Maddich
From: Rosie Edwards
Subject: Way to go, Mom

Wow, Mom – Europe!!! To say that you surprised me would be an understatement. I'm so happy for you. Have a great time. Keep the emails coming. I want to hear all about it.

I'm sure you've heard from Dennis by now. He's doing his usual ranting and raving. "How could she do this? This is terrible!" Well, you get the picture. But, don't pay any attention to him. You just keep having fun with Katherine.

I wish I could be there with you. It will be a few years before Carl and I can afford a European vacation. Take lots of pictures. Can't wait until your next email.

Love, Rosie

CHAPTER 3

Ivan Borovsky was a very wealthy man. He was also a man to be feared. His ruthlessness and cunning, learned while growing up on the streets of Moscow in the former Soviet Union, made him what he was today – a Russian arms dealer.

He learned early on that only the strongest survived. The weak perished. He started by stealing food when he was five years old so he and his mother wouldn't starve. One day Boris, a bully in the neighborhood, cornered him on his way home. Ivan was too small to defend himself. Boris punched him and knocked him to the ground. Then he stole the food Ivan was bringing home. When he got home, he cried as he told his mother what had happened.

She slapped him across the face. "Stop crying. Stop being a baby," she said to him. "Learn from this. Keep

Boris's name in your mind. Some day, you will be big like him. And, when you are, then you will get your revenge for what he has done to you today. For now, stay out of his way."

By the time he was twelve years old, Ivan had branched out with the help of his mother. He trusted no one except her. He was now known as the "go to guy" in the neighborhood. For a fee or a swap when someone wanted hard-to-come-by items like soap, toilet paper, light blubs or cosmetics, people went to Ivan. People knew he could get what they wanted.

His mother had a job as a cleaning lady at one of the better hotels in Moscow. All employees were checked as they left work each evening to prevent theft. Over time, she was able to learn the locations of all the back entrances and underground passageways in the building. She studied the schedules of when the many suppliers made their deliveries and when the security people made their rounds. Since she could not bring stolen goods out of the hotel herself, she would stash small amounts of hotel supplies in her cleaning cart and then hide them in various out-of-the-way places like the boiler room. She sewed false pockets in Ivan's coat. She drew him a map of the layout of the hotel. Then, once a week, she would make sure a back door was left unlocked so Ivan could enter, go to her hiding places and bring out the goods.

During this time, Ivan never forgot Boris, the bully who beat him up when he was five years old. Boris still lived in the neighborhood, but he amounted to nothing more than a shiftless drunk who could only terrorize people with his size rather than his brains. One night, Boris made a fatal mistake. He broke into Ivan's apartment and stole all the money Ivan had been accumulating in his small business. If he had kept his mouth shut about the break in, no one would have known who committed the crime. But Boris couldn't resist boasting about what he had done. He flashed the money around in a neighborhood tavern. Word got back to Ivan who was now fourteen years old.

"Now you must do something about Boris," his mother said when Ivan told her what happened. "Your business is small yet, but you must have respect. Never appear weak. You must kill Boris and make sure everyone knows it was you who did it. Once you do that, no one will dare bother you again."

Ivan carried a knife and followed Boris for five days watching to see when he was the most vulnerable. Boris made it easy, since he went to the tavern and got drunk every night. Now that he had Ivan's money, he was able to buy not shots but bottles of vodka. There wasn't a night he didn't stagger home.

Ivan knew he had to catch Boris by surprise, since he was still smaller than him. He knew he couldn't attack him from the front. Even drunk, Boris would be able to grab him and easily take his knife away. But stabbing people in the back was useless too because of all the bones. No damage could be done unless you knew where and how to slide the knife between a person's ribs. Ivan didn't. Therefore, when Boris stumbled by the entrance to the alley that night, Ivan stepped out and plunged the blade of his knife into the side of Boris' neck. It entered the jugular vein causing Boris to bleed out in minutes.

Ivan waited until the body stopped twitching before he dug into Boris's pockets and pulled out a few rubles. He shoved them into his mouth to let people know the reason for his death. Ivan felt nothing as he walked away.

His business grew over the years, until finally he got the attention of the Russian Mafia. Ivan was smart enough to know his best chance was not to fight them but to join them. He hated being a part of the Mafia. Mafia people were nothing but thugs like Boris – peasants who had no class. He had bigger plans for his future. Many times he wanted to walk away. However, it was his mother who could see his potential and told him to bide his time.

Ivan was certain of two things. The Soviet Union was going to fall, and when it did the person holding the weapons and the cash would be the most powerful. Without the knowledge of the Mafia, he began buying or stealing weapons whenever and wherever he could. He stored them in a secret warehouse he had in the Soviet countryside. Slowly he began to move the weapons to a cave along the Southern border of Russia. Since the banking system in the Soviet Union was nonexistent, he also exchanged his rubles for American dollars at every opportunity and kept them hidden.

When the fall of the Soviet Union came, he was ready. He and his mother left for Helsinki, and from there he went to Paris where he still lived today. Other than retrieving his stash of guns from the cave in the South, Ivan never entered Russia again.

He started his gun business dealing with small time gangsters and street gangs in the European cities. But he was farsighted enough to see the real money and the power lay in supplying arms to the various rebel and terrorist groups throughout the world. To do this, he knew he needed to hire people who could help his organization grow. The one thing he looked for and insisted on was that his employees have brains along with the muscle, because the Boris's of the world were small-time punks and nothing more. Anyone who worked for him had to have completed all grades in public school. His second in command was Dimitri Zarenko, a university graduate.

Ivan's mother chose to live in a large flat in London in the more expensive part of the city. She thought Paris was too small and crowded. She also had Ivan bring her sister out of Russia so she wouldn't be lonely. He did as she asked. As powerful as he had become, Ivan still trusted only his mother. He always used her as his go-between for all of his arms deals. The buyers would have to deliver their payments to her first before he would deliver the weapons to them. Ivan didn't trust anyone but her to handle the transfer of cash. When a deal was going down, his mother and aunt would travel to the payoff site to collect the cash. Once done, they would then contact Ivan so he could complete the transaction. In the beginning, a few groups refused to go along with it. They wanted the cash and the weapons to be handed over at the same time. Ivan saw to it that their money was taken and their go-betweens ended up dead. It only took a few times until everyone who dealt with Ivan knew they had to make their payments to his mother.

Check Out Receipt

West Bend Community Memorial Library
262-335-5151
www.west-bendlibrary.org

Monday, March 4, 2019 10:09:48 AM
61828

Item: 33357004882699
Title: My mother rebels
Material: Book
Due: 04/01/2019

Total items: 1

Thank You!

CHAPTER 4

Remember when I said it was uncanny how a random event in one place could affect the outcome of a random event in another place? Here in the United States if the three of us hadn't tried to make our mother sell her house, she wouldn't have gotten angry and taken off for Europe with Pauline - the first random event.

The second event in this scenario occurred in Europe. And, because of it, my mother and Pauline became involved in an international arms deal.

Ivan's mother and aunt were in a London taxi on their way to the train station. They were traveling from London to Paris to collect payment for yet another of Ivan's arms deals. In order to reach Paris they were going to be traveling by train on the Eurostar via the Channel Tunnel or "Chunnel" which runs under the English Channel.

At this same time, my mother and Pauline were also in a London taxi on their way to the same train station. They too were planning to travel from London to Paris on the Eurostar via the Chunnel.

My mother's taxi reached the train station without any problems. However, the taxi carrying Ivan's mother and aunt broke down in traffic causing the two of them to miss their scheduled train to Paris – hence, the European random event.

"The two women just left their flat and are in a taxi on their way to the train station. They will be traveling on the Eurostar leaving at nine o'clock this morning. Look for them in the Business Premier class. They have tickets for seats one and three in compartment A." This was the phone message given to the African gentleman standing on the platform in the train station. He ended the call without saying a word. He would dispose of this cell phone when he reached Paris and then buy a new one for the arms deal with Ivan Borovsky. To prevent any tracking, he made it a practice never to use any phone for more than five calls before getting rid of it.

He boarded the Eurostar for Paris and took his seat in Coach class. He was dressed in a conservative, dark blue, pinstriped suit, one of many he still had from his days at Oxford. He needed to look the part, because later he would be walking through the Business class to check out the two women. When he handed over the diamonds later today in Paris, he wanted to be sure who they were. He allowed nothing to chance.

He was an agent representing a group of rebels fighting a war in Zaire. This was how he made his living. He traveled around the world brokering deals for the various warring factions throughout Africa. Most of the members of the rebel groups were just street punks trying to gain power in their respective countries. None of them were intellectually capable of making deals for toothpaste let alone weapons. In addition, they would stick out like sore thumbs if they came to Europe themselves. They would be watched the minute they set foot on the Continent. That's why they all needed someone like him. His Oxford education gave him the polish to travel anywhere without causing suspicion. It also gave him the tools to be a good negotiator.

CHAPTER 5

"I think this is it," Katherine said. She checked the seating numbers on the outside of the Business Premier class, Compartment A on the Eurostar. "Our seats are two and four, right? See, they're the two next to the door. Seats one and three are the ones next to the window," she added pointing to the legend on the outside panel. The two women entered the compartment and stored their bags in the side closet.

Once they were settled Pauline said, "Oh, what a treat England has been. I hope our trip continues to be just as wonderful. I'm so glad you suggested we travel to the countryside instead of staying in London. We never would've experienced the flavor of England if we hadn't. Sort of like foreigners coming to New York and saying they visited America."

The train started to pull out of the station. "Looks like we've got the compartment to ourselves. Let's take the two seats next to the window," Katherine said as she moved over. "If anyone does come, we'll just move back. You know, Pauline, I know you're not comfortable about going into the Chunnel. Is that why you booked these expensive tickets in Business class? You think we're going to be any safer in here if something goes wrong under the English Channel?"

"No. I booked them because you're the one who booked us into the George Cinq Hotel in Paris, for crying out loud. I figured if we're going to run out of money after we pay the bill at that swanky hotel, we might as well arrive in Paris in style," Pauline answered.

"I explained that. Since we've both been to Paris twice and have seen almost all the major tourist sights there are to see, we're only going to be in the hotel for two nights. I booked the cheapest room the hotel has. And besides, I always wanted to be able to say, *when I was staying at the George Cinq . . .*" Katherine said in a snooty voice and smiled at her friend. "We'll do the Youth Hostels for the rest of our trip."

When the train came out of the Chunnel on the French side, Katherine and Pauline were busy looking out the window at all the pear and apple trees in bloom.

This part of northern France was known for these types of fruit trees. They didn't notice the African gentleman looking into their compartment as he walked past.

Earlier that morning, Tony Cappelli, the CIA agent stationed at the American Embassy in Paris, received a coded memo informing him of the suspected arms deal going down involving Ivan Borovsky. Police organizations around the world had been after Borovsky for years. But because of the many layers between him and his purchasers, no one was ever able to catch him. Just recently however, Interpol uncovered the fact that Ivan always used his mother and his aunt as the go-between in all of his deals. They were the ones who collected the payments before Ivan would turn over the weapons.

Per the memo, Ivan's mother and aunt were on their way to Paris right now. Their train was due to arrive at one o'clock today. When they were in the city, they always stayed at the George Cinq Hotel, the luxury hotel off the Champs-Elysées. It was within walking distance from the American Embassy.

Tony headed for his boss's office down the hall. "We just received this memo," Tony said when he entered the room. "Look's like Borovsky's about to pull another arms deal. It may be right here in Paris, because his mother and aunt are on their way here. My contact at Interpol says they have a reservation at the George Cinq. I plan to walk over there this afternoon and keep an eye on them. If we nab those two ladies right at the payoff site, we just might put a huge hole in Borovsky's operation, since he refuses to allow anyone but his mother and her sister to pick up the money."

CHAPTER 6

After they were checked in at the hotel, Katherine and Pauline discovered just how small the cheapest room at the George Cinq really was. "Good grief," Pauline said. "The only good thing I can say about this tiny room is that at least we have a view of the Champs-Elysées. After we unpack and freshen up, let's get out of here and have a cup of coffee at an outdoor café. I don't think there's enough oxygen in here to sustain us for more than an hour."

Later when they had exited the hotel and were on their way to an outdoor café, Katherine asked, "Which way should we go? Left or right?"

Pauline looked around and pointed across the street. "How about we go to that café with the red awning across the street?"

Neither realized they had just chosen the most notoriously, expensive café in Paris. As they crossed the wide boulevard, they were unaware they were being watched by the man from the train. Nor did they realize the café they chose was the actual site of where the payoff for the arms deal was to take place.

Since this was a warm spring day, they sat down at an outside table near the ornate fence along the sidewalk. They were mesmerized by the hustle and bustle of the people walking by.

Pauline smiled and said, "Isn't it amazing how countries around the world take on specific personalities that define everything about the country from the architecture to the environment and even the people? For example, for me England brought thoughts of steadfastness, being solid, and no frills. Think about it. Their castles were plain and substantial, very little rococo inside or out. Their food was hardy with little seasoning. They're known, not for delicate wines, but heavy ales. Even the British people have reserved personalities, not like the Italians who are emotional and emphasize every sentence with their hands."

"I never thought of that, Pauline," Katherine said. "But I think you're right. Look at France," she said sweeping her hand down the boulevard. "I would say this country is arty, frilly, and light. Look at the ornate, iron railings on the buildings across the street. Even the Eiffel Tower is constructed with intricate latticework. French food is fancy and delicate. The language pronunciations are soft with few harsh sounds. And, think of their artwork as opposed to the English, light and airy like Monet and his water lilies. Hmm, I like traveling with you," Katherine smiled at her friend. "You see things and make me think."

Pauline was nodding her head. "By the way, speaking of the Eiffel Tower, isn't it something only a little over one hundred years ago, the Eiffel Tower was the tallest structure on the Planet? Now with all the skyscrapers in every country, it seems hard to believe, doesn't it?"

Their waiter arrived to take their order. They only wanted coffee so neither bothered to look at a menu. When the coffee was served, Katherine took her first sip. It was then she happened to glance up at the large menu posted next to the inside door of the café.

"You have got to be kidding." She set her cup down with a clink. "The sign near the door says a cup of coffee costs twenty Euros. That's about thirty American dollars!"

"Oh, come on. Put your glasses on. You must have misread the sign," Pauline said as she turned to read it.

Just then the gentleman from Africa sat down in one of the empty chairs at their table and laid a small box next to Katherine. It appeared to be nailed shut. Both women were startled by the man's behavior.

"Here is the payment for the exchange. You can now contact your son and tell him you have received it," he said in a hushed voice.

"What?" both women said in unison.

"My son?" Katherine was completely baffled by the stranger's behavior.

He then handed her a folder piece of paper. "You must also give him this. It is the new phone number where I can be reached to complete the transaction. I expect him to call me within the hour." Then the man stood up.

"Sir," Katherine picked up the box wanting to return it to him. It was quite heavy.

"Sir, I think you have . . ." But before Pauline could finish her sentence of "the wrong people," the man had already walked away.

Palms up, in a helpless gesture, Pauline asked, "What the heck just happened?"

"I don't know. But that was creepy. Do you think we should get out of here, Pauline?" Katherine put the box in her purse and started to rise.

"Hold it," Pauline said. "I don't care how creepy that was, we just paid sixty bucks for these two cups of coffee. I'm not leaving until I finish mine." She picked up her cup and finished it off in one swallow, then scrunched her nose and added, "Big deal. It just tastes like regular coffee to me." She grabbed her purse and said, "Okay. Now let's get the heck out of here." She motioned to the waiter to bring their check.

After they paid their bill, they hurried out of the café. They were standing with a crowd of people at the curb waiting for the light to change. "What do you think we should do?" Pauline asked.

"Well, I did say I wanted to have an adventure. Looks like we got into a doozie this time."

"That's not even funny, Kiddo."

"I think this is some kind of weird set up, Pauline. I still can't believe what just happened."

"And, what's with that box? What do you think is in there? Is it heavy?" Pauline asked.

"Well, it's not light. Look, as soon as we get back to our room, I think we should open it and see what's inside," Katherine answered.

CHAPTER 7

Tony Cappelli was standing at the curb across the street from George Cinq waiting for the light to change. He had been taking up various positions around the hotel for the past two hours waiting for Ivan's mother and aunt to arrive. So far nothing. The two ladies hadn't shown up. Maybe Interpol got this wrong. Maybe there was no arms deal going down, he thought.

The conversation between two women standing directly behind him broke into his consciousness because of the sounds he was hearing. It was funny no matter where he traveled in the world if someone spoke English with an American accent he picked up on it. It never happened to him at other times when the accent was from a different country, but these two women, whoever they were, really stood out. It wasn't their words so much that caught his ear at first. It was their horrible accents. They definitely have to be somewhere from the upper Mid-West with all the flat vowel sounds they're uttering. And, how many people use words like *doozie* and *kiddo* except actual Americans, he thought.

The light changed. He stepped off the curb and proceeded across the street. He decided to make one more walk by before actually entering the hotel to sit in the lobby. Reconnoitering in the lobby wasn't the best thing to do because there was always a strong possibility of arousing the suspicion of the house detectives.

The ladies couldn't get the door to their room open, closed, and locked fast enough. Katherine took the box out of her purse and laid it on the bed. It was about eight inches long and three inches deep, sort of like a cigar box. It was nailed shut. The two of them just stood and looked at it for a moment without saying a word.

"What do you think is in there?" Pauline asked softly. "What if it's something dangerous, like poison or biological chemicals?"

Katherine picked up the box and shook it. She could hear muffled tinkling sounds. Then she shook it again so Pauline could hear it. "Well, the tinkling doesn't sound like it can be poisons or chemicals. And, we aren't going to know until we open it, are we?" She laid it back on the bed.

They stood for a few more minutes staring down at it. "Oh, nuts to this. Let's get this over with. I'll use my Swiss Army knife to wedge it open," Katherine said and went to her suitcase to retrieve the knife.

"We're from the old school," she told Pauline. "We wouldn't think of traveling abroad without a Swiss Army knife or a Leatherman tool kit. Now days, the younger generation wouldn't think of traveling without a cell phone or an iPad." She opened her knife and held it up. "Hah, let them try to open a nailed-shut box with those gadgets and see where it gets them."

When she wedged the top off of the box, they saw it contained a large, black drawstring bag. Again, both women stood there without moving.

"This is getting us nowhere," Pauline said disgustedly. She took the bag out of the box. Whatever was in there cascaded to the bottom of the bag. It sounded like pebbles. She put the plump bag on the bed and worked to untie the strings. Once opened, when she turned it upside down. Dozens and dozens and dozens of milky rocks of varying sizes fell out onto the bed. Some were somewhat shinny and bright most were hazy and dull.

Each of them picked up a pebble and examined it. Pauline turned the stone over in her hand. "This looks like a large pile of rock salt. What do you think these are?"

"Beats me." Katherine answered. "The man said the box was payment for an exchange, whatever that means. But, these don't look like ordinary rocks, do they?" She picked up a bunch of the stones and let them cascade through her fingers. "Some of them seem to sparkle. Have you ever seen raw diamonds? Do you think that's what these are?"

"Oh, come on. Raw diamonds? Don't get dramatic on me," Pauline said as she began to put the rocks back into the bag. "But I have to say, this whole thing has been weird. It's giving me the creeps. And what about that phone number the man gave you. No way are we going to call it. What if this is a set up to kidnap Americans and then use us as ransom for a trade for terrorists being held at Guantanamo?"

"Pauline! Now who's being dramatic? But, all the same, let's not stay in Paris for the two days. This just doesn't feel right. Let's get out of here early tomorrow morning, okay? We've been here before. We've seen all the highlights of this city."

"No argument from me," Pauline answered. "You know what? I think it would be better if we didn't leave the hotel tonight either. We'll just have dinner in one of the restaurants here. And, then tomorrow we'll rent a car and leave. Let's go up to Holland. My Dutch grandmother would spin in her grave if I didn't visit that country, and, it's really not very far of a drive."

CHAPTER 8

After he crossed the street, Tony Cappelli walked down one block and stood next to the entrance of an apartment building while he kept an eye on the hotel. He saw a taxi pull up to the entrance of the George Cinq. The two women got out who matched the pictures he had in the file of Borovsky's mother and aunt. One of the women was on a cell phone. She looked agitated. He also spotted his Interpol contact, Henri, walking past the taxi and into the hotel. He decided it was time to approach the hotel. He picked up his pace as he walked.

Henri was already seated in a chair next to the window when he walked into the lobby. He took the seat next to him.

The two women were now at the desk checking in. "Is that Borovsky's mother?" he asked his colleague quietly.

"Yes. And apparently something has gone wrong. My Russian isn't that good, but when I passed their taxi I heard one of the women say something about a missed train. She seemed very upset," Henri said softly. "I'm going to stay awhile to see what happens."

"Good idea. I'll join you if you don't mind?" Tony took a newspaper out of his coat pocket and opened it. He kept a watch on the two women as they checked in and left the lobby for their rooms.

In the late afternoon, neither of them paid any attention to Katherine and Pauline as they got off the elevator and went to the Concierge Desk. After a few minutes, the Concierge handed Pauline a piece of paper and then pointed to the restaurant on the other side of the lobby.

On their way to the restaurant, Pauline said, "I feel better knowing we're going to get out of here." She folded the rental car agreement the Concierge had given them and put it in her purse. "I don't know what it is about you, Katherine, but every time I do things with you, we get into trouble."

"Hey!" Katherine said. "This one wasn't my fault. And, it's all going to be over tomorrow morning anyway. Once we're out of here, we can enjoy the rest of our vacation."

Oh, the flat-vowel American ladies again, Tony thought as the two women passed him. He looked up over the top of his newspaper and watched the backs of them as they walked toward the entrance to the restaurant. Definitely, upper-Midwest.

By early evening, Borovsky's mother and aunt still hadn't left the hotel nor did they even come down for dinner.

"I don't know what's going on." Tony checked his watch. "I think I'm going to call it a day." He stood up.

"I agree," Henri answered as he rose from his chair. "I wonder what was so important about missing a train though. Ah, well, another wasted day. I will wait outside for my night man to show up. Then I plan on going home too. I will keep you informed if I hear anything."

CHAPTER 9

The African agent just got off the phone with Dimitri Zarenko, Ivan's second-in-command. He learned he had given the diamonds to the wrong women. Eight hundred thousand Euros in diamonds to the wrong women! All because Ivan had some sort of Oedipus complex with his mother. He told Dimitri this was all Ivan's fault, which he firmly believed.

But, then in his anger, he told Dimitri how he had Ivan's mother and aunt followed all the way from their flat in London. That was a big mistake, because now he was positive he was a marked man. He knew Ivan would come after him not only for giving the diamonds to the wrong ladies, but, more importantly, for knowing where his mother lived and then following her in London.

What to do? What to do, he thought. His first thought was to return to the George Cinq to see if he could find the two women and get the diamonds back. But, he was quite sure Ivan would already have his men planted at the hotel to protect his mother. If any of Ivan's thugs spotted him, it would all be over. He also knew unless the diamonds were found and the deal went through, there was no way he could go back to Africa. Because he brokered so many arms deals there, once the word went out that he failed, it would spread like wild fire. He wouldn't be safe anywhere on that continent. And, Europe was too small a place to try to hide. As an African, he would stick out no matter what city he ran to. Borovsky was sure to find him.

For now, he would remain in his hotel room, order room service, and use the time to think.

CHAPTER 10

Dimitri Zarenko was not looking forward to the meeting with his boss. Ivan had called him earlier in the day informing him that his mother and aunt missed the Eurostar, because the London taxi had broken down. Ivan wanted him to call the agent to arrange a new meeting place for the transfer of the diamonds. But, the problem was Dimitri didn't know how to contact the man about the screw-up, because he didn't have the man's current phone number. This was the first time he worked with the shifty African agent. But, it was well known he kept changing cell phones; and he always delivered his newest number for each transaction.

Fifteen minutes ago the agent had called him. He demanded to know why no one had contacted him about delivery of the weapons, since he had delivered the diamonds as instructed and given the two ladies his new phone number. When Dimitri told him about the missed train, the agent started yelling and accusing Ivan of thievery. He added the fact that his partner in London saw the women leave their apartment and get in a taxi on their way to the train station. He personally observed them on the Eurostar in the correct seats. He knew they always stayed at the George Cinq. He watched the women as they went to the correct café across the street from the hotel for the rendezvous. He did everything he was told to do on his end. It was Ivan who was trying to cheat him by making up a story that his mother missed the train. It was Ivan who was going to pay for this.

Dimitri was dumbfounded – first because the agent even knew Ivan's mother lived in London; and worse, he had the gall to have her followed. How did he even know they stayed at the George Cinq when they came to Paris? If this idiot knew these things about Ivan's mother, how many more people knew? He had been after Ivan for months now to stop using his mother and aunt for the payment part of the deals. He should have listened, he thought. He dreaded having to tell Ivan about this.

If that wasn't enough, the agent added one more thing. If Ivan didn't complete the arms deal and deliver the weapons within forty-eight hours, he was going to put the word out on the street about how Ivan cheated him. He said Ivan was getting too old. He needed to be replaced. The idea of having to involve his mother in each and every arms deal was ludicrous.

"Well, did you arrange a new drop point for the cash?" Ivan asked Dimitri as soon as he entered Ivan's apartment.

"I could not contact him, because this is the guy who changes cell phones every two minutes. I had to wait until he contacted me," Dimitri replied. "You are not going to like this, Ivan. The guy said he did deliver the diamonds to two, older women at the café. Now he wants his weapons."

"What are you talking about? No diamonds have been delivered. My Mother missed her train."

"That is just it. He said there *were* two, older women on the train from London sitting in the exact seats that were assigned to your mother and aunt. Not only that, those women checked into the George Cinq when they arrived in Paris. And they even ended up going to the correct café. Apparently, he gave the diamonds to them thinking they were your mother and aunt. Or at least that is what he told me," Dimitri said.

"How did the *schwartzer* even know my mother lived in London? How did he know what train they would be on or that they stayed at the George Cinq when they came to Paris?" Ivan asked very quietly.

There was a grim look on Dimitri's face. He blew out a breath of air and pursed his lips. Might as well get this over with he thought. "He had your mother followed from London. He was on the Eurostar they were supposed to be traveling on. He knew the number of their assigned seats. When he checked their compartment, he said there were two older women sitting in those seats. He assumed they were your mother and aunt."

"He followed my mother all the way from London?" Ivan roared. "He knew where they lived? How? How did he know these things? I want him dead, Dimitri. You kill him. By the end of today, I want him gone. Dead, Dimitri. And don't just shoot him in the head. Start with the knees and slowly work your way up to his brain. I want him to know exactly why you are killing him." Ivan's face was almost purple, he was so furious.

Dimitri stood there for a moment and rubbed his brow. He felt a headache coming on. He knew he wouldn't be able to reason with Ivan when he was like this. He really should have stopped using his mother long ago. It was just a matter of time before something like this happened.

"All right, Ivan. I will find this man for you and have him killed. But, we also have to find those two women who have the diamonds. I am going to use the German kid to see if he can find out who else had tickets on the Eurostar. That should be easy for him to hack into the train's computer," Dimitri said.

It took Dimitri over a year to convince Ivan to add a computer person to his payroll. But, Ivan was from the old school. He couldn't see any need for technology. And, because the kid was German and not Russian, Ivan was even more suspicious of hiring him.

"No. First you kill the African. That is the first thing you need to do. And, I do not trust that *Kraut*. This should be between you and me. I do not want anyone else knowing my business. I have told you that many times," Ivan said. "One more thing, tomorrow morning, I want you personally to escort my mother and aunt to the train station. Then assign one of our men to meet them in London and escort them to their home." He seemed calmer, but his hands were still balled into fists as he glared at Dimitri.

"All right. I will call you when it is all over," Dimitri said just before he left the room. The best thing now was to leave and let Ivan calm down, he thought. I know Ivan wants me personally to kill the agent. But, I have too much planning to do. Once we locate where the agent is holed-up, I will call in some of our men for help.

Whether Ivan wanted it or not, Dimitri knew his best bet in finding the agent and the two women was going to be getting Helmut involved. That nineteen year-old kid was a genius on the computer. He lived to hack into various computer systems. As long as he could be at his computer, he wasn't interested in anything else.

When Dimitri first met him, he was living in a dump. He had very few furnishings and almost no food in his refrigerator. He spent every dime, his own and other people's whose identity he had stolen, on computer equipment. One of the first things Dimitri did was move Helmut to a better location and then pay him a decent salary so he no longer had to steal identities for every new gadget that came along. He didn't want him to be arrested for something as stupid as identity theft.

Right after Dimitri hired him, Helmut changed the routing on all electronic correspondence coming into and leaving Ivan's business. That way things sent and received had became almost untraceable. Just that alone was worth any amount Ivan could have paid him. He was sure the kid would be able to find out where the agent was located. And, hacking into the Eurostar system to find out who those two women were would be simple for him.

CHAPTER 11

Early the next morning while they were packing, Pauline held up the box of stones and asked, "What are we going to do with this? Should we just leave it here?"

"No. Let's take it with us as a memento of our first European adventure. We can pull these things out when we get back home as we embellish the story of what happened to us in Paris," Katherine laughed. She took the box from Pauline and put it in her tote bag.

At eight-thirty the front desk called informing them their rental car had arrived. In truth, the two of them had had their bags packed and were ready to go since six o'clock that morning. They wouldn't feel safe until they were out of Paris. They rolled their suitcases to the elevator and went down to the lobby.

After the hotel bill was settled, they picked up the keys to their car. Because the two hotel doormen were busy unloading the car of an arriving guest, a gentleman entering the hotel to pick up his boss's mother and aunt held the door for them as they were leaving. Their black Volvo rental car was parked at the end of the circular drive.

Pauline won the coin toss for who would drive out of Paris. She was happy about that, since Katherine drove like a *ditz head* when she was in a new city. Right now, they did not need any more stress, she thought. They did not need some old man yell "Move your *bloomin arse*" like the man in England did. Of course, here in Paris the old guy would probably yell, "Move your *derriere, s'il vous plait.*" She smiled at that thought.

Before setting off, she programmed the GPS for Amsterdam.

"I checked out the weather in Holland, no rain and temperatures in the mid-sixties. Hopefully, the tulips will be starting to bloom. This should be a good time to be there." She pulled out onto the Champs-Elysees and headed northwest.

Once outside of the city limits, Katherine studied the foldout map of the route they would be taking. After a few minutes, she said, "Hey, you know what? We're going to drive right through Antwerp. It's supposed to be the diamond capital of the world."

She looked over at Pauline and shrugged her shoulders. "As long as we're going through there, why don't we stop at one of those diamond places and see if these stones really are diamonds?

"What do you mean diamonds?" Pauline snorted as she glanced at her friend. "We don't even know what those things are. They still look like rock salt if you ask me. How dumb will we look when the jeweler tells us they're just paste? Come on . . ."

Katherine continued to study the map. She began tracing the route they would have to take to Antwerp. It was as if she wasn't even listening to Pauline. "We'll each take one of the sparkly ones for them to look at. Tell them we bought them at a stall in a Paris street market for two hundred bucks and want to know if we got cheated. They'll never see us again. What have we got to lose?" Katherine pulled the box out of her tote bag and began digging around looking for two stones that actually looked like diamonds.

"Ha." She held up two medium size stones. "Look at these. They look sparkly."

Pauline knew she wouldn't be able to talk Katherine out of this. "All right. We'll stop in Antwerp," she said reluctantly.

When they neared Antwerp, Pauline got off the freeway to enter the city. Meanwhile, Katherine googled the stores that offered diamond appraisals. The district was enormous. It covered approximately one square mile in the city. It took them another forty minutes just to reach the diamond district and locate the store Katherine had chosen.

For a moment after they parked, they just sat in the car and looked at the stores and the hustle and bustle of the people on the street. "You sure you want to do this?" Pauline asked as she studied the various jewelry stores. "Look at the bars on all the windows and the security gizmos on the doors. I don't think you should keep the box in your bag when we go in. We'd probably set off alarms just walking into the place."

"You're right," Katherine said as pocketed her diamond and handed the other one to Pauline. She removed the box from her tote bag, turned, and laid it on the back seat.

"Okay. Let's go."

The store they chose, *Abraham and Sons*, was located in the middle of the block. Even though it was a small establishment, from the outside it seemed to be equipped with the latest electronic security. Along with finding the store on Google, Katherine also read since 2003 when a gang of five Italians stole hundreds of millions of dollars in diamonds from a safety deposit vault regarded as impenetrable, electronic security was beefed up in every business in this area.

The mood was very somber as they entered. Cameras seemed to be everywhere throughout the store. All the workers in the store were Orthodox Jews. Along with wearing yarmulkes, beards and long side curls, they were also wearing the traditional, long black wool coats called *rekels*. Other than Katherine and Pauline, there were no other women in the store. For a moment, no one moved. The workers just stared at the women. Finally, an old man working at a table behind the counter looked up. He smiled at the women as he stood and walked to the counter.

"May I help you, Mesdames," he said in English.

They returned the gentleman's smile as they approached him. Katherine laid her stone on the counter. "We would like our stones appraised. Truthfully, we don't even know what they are."

Pauline then added her stone. "We bought these at a street market in Paris. The vendor told us they were diamonds, but we're not sure if they are. We need to know if these are real diamonds, or did we get taken? Was this a scam?"

"*Nu*, let us see what you have," the jeweler said as he adjusted his eye loupe and picked up Katherine's stone first. He was quiet as he examined the gem. He set it down and picked up Pauline's stone. While he was turning her stone in his fingers, he asked, "Where did you say you purchased these stones?"

"At a stall in one of those street markets in Paris," Katherine answered while looking at Pauline for confirmation.

Pauline nodded her head. "Yeah, it was one of those street stalls." She squinted her eyes and pursed her lips at Katherine as if to say, you are getting us into another idiotic mess. Katherine gave a slight shrug and looked back at the jeweler.

He had taken the loupe from his eye and seemed to be studying the two women. "How much did you pay for these stones," he asked.

"Two hundred dollars," Katherine answered before Pauline could open her mouth.

"You paid in American dollars?" he asked as he looked up at the women.

"Oh, ah, no, I meant Euros, two hundred Euros," Katherine replied quickly. "I'm sorry, I always say dollars instead of Euros," she added with a weak laugh. "My fault." Why did she start to feel nervous?

"Why did you choose these particular stones?" he asked opening his hand over the two stones on the counter.

"They were the biggest ones he had," Pauline chimed in. "You know how Americans are. We always have to have the biggest of everything." Katherine nodded her head at that one.

Now it was the jeweler's turn to slowly nod his head at them as he continued to stare silently. By now the other workers in the store had stopped what they were doing and concentrated on what was taking place at the counter. The two of them could feel the change in the air.

Pauline swallowed and looked at Katherine out of the corner of her eye. Katherine ran her tongue over her bottom lip. They could hear the tick of the clock on the wall. It was so quiet.

Katherine, being the more impatient of the two, blurted out, "Okay. What's going on? These are just rocks aren't they? We got taken. We're just two foolish old women, right?"

"Well, Mesdames," the Jeweler began. "It seems you have a good *American* eye." He nodded to Pauline when he said this. "They are indeed diamonds; and they have a value of around three thousand Euros each."

"That's about four thousand American dollars, depending on the exchange rate," he added with a smile as he watched Katherine try to do the conversion in her head.

"Four thousands dollars each? Each?" Pauline squeaked. The jeweler flipped his hand back and forth indicating both had the same approximate value.

"You've got to be kidding?" Katherine whispered staring down at the diamonds. She turned to her friend and mouthed, Oh my God!

"Are you vacationing here in Antwerp?" the jeweler asked as he reached for the pad to write up the receipt for the appraisal.

Without thinking, Pauline answered, "No. We just stopped in Antwerp for an appraisal on our way to Amsterdam." She winced after she said this. For some reason, she thought telling the man where they would be going was a mistake.

He continued to fill out the receipts and had his head down. "Amsterdam. I see. Are you planning to stay in Amsterdam for any length of time?" he asked quietly.

The way the jeweler continued to question them made them even more uneasy. They wanted to leave. Katherine picked up her diamond and put it in her purse before the jeweler could put it into the customary small bag he had on the counter. Pauline followed suit. Both had their charge cards out ready to settle the bill before he even had the receipts finished. They felt an overwhelming urge to get out of that store.

Once on the street, they quickly walked back to their car. "Good grief, Katherine. What have we gotten ourselves into here? It got so uncomfortable in the store. What was that all about? And, if these two diamonds are worth over seven thousand dollars alone, what is the whole bag worth? Think about this, if that man in Paris really was trying to con us, why would he give us a gazillion dollars in real diamonds!"

"I don't think it was a con, Pauline. But, whatever it was, I don't think it was good. And, I agree with you. What's up with the jeweler asking us those questions about where we're staying?" Katherine added.

Then she stopped and grabbed Pauline's arm. "Oh, no. The box! I just left it sitting in plain sight on the back seat of our car!"

Their heads popped up. Both looked down the street at their parked car. Without breaking into a run, they picked up the pace.

Katherine began panting. They were going so fast. "Does it look like our car has been broken into?"

"No. But don't stop now," Pauline said just as breathlessly. It seemed impossible two old ladies could walk that fast.

Katherine put her hand on her heart when they reached the car and spotted the box right where she had left it. "Oh, thank goodness. It's still there,"

As soon as the women left the store, the jeweler came around the counter. He stood at the window and silently watched them hurry down the street. He tapped his nose. "Something is not right about those two," he said. "I can sense it. No one would be selling raw diamonds like that in a street stall no matter what city it was." When they reached their car, he wrote down their license plate number.

"Didn't we receive an international alert about stolen diamonds from Africa last week?" he asked his co-workers. "I think a phone call to Interpol about those two Americans wouldn't hurt."

CHAPTER 12

EMAIL
From: Jane Atkins
To: Katherine Wilson

I am enjoying your emails about what you and Pauline have been up to. And, of course, when I begin to read them I get all weepy. You know me.

I was so surprised to hear that you left Paris after only one day and are on your way to Amsterdam. I thought you were going to stay for 2 or 3 days and try to see things off the beaten tourist path that you haven't seen before. Amsterdam seems like an interesting city. But, if I had to choose, I would love to be in Paris. Listen to me talk. With the kids being so young, it will be years before Jeff and I are able to make decisions like that. For now I am touring Europe vicariously through your eyes, so keep the emails coming.

Emily is doing so well in kindergarten. She can hardly wait for the bus to pick her up each day. Even though she has been in school for months now, I still miss her and can't wait until she gets home. The twins are doing great in nursery school. They are finally starting to play with other kids and not just with each other. When they start kindergarten, I may see if they can be put into separate classes so they have a chance to grow individually. But, maybe not. Maybe twins need to be together. I have to read more articles on twins to make sure I am doing the right thing.

Well, Mom, have fun in Amsterdam. Write soon.

Love, Jane

Katherine and Pauline arrived in Amsterdam late in the afternoon. Katherine held onto the box of diamonds without letting go once all the way from Antwerp. Her fingers were cramped by the time they reached the new city. While traveling from Paris, they had booked a room at a hotel in the heart of the city. Before they pulled up to the hotel, she stuffed the box down to the bottom of her tote bag. When they got out of the car, she held the tote bag so tight under her arm the entire Dutch army wouldn't have been able to pry it loose. As they walked to the entrance, she looked up and down the street keeping surveillance on their surroundings. The CIA would have been proud of her.

"Would you knock it off," Pauline hissed as they were checking in. "Your cloak-and-dagger act looks ridiculous. It's going to call attention to us."

"We can't be too careful," Katherine whispered making another sweep of the lobby and squeezing the bag even tighter against her chest. Pauline let out a breath of air and rolled her eyes.

Once in their room, they locked the door. Katherine took the box of diamonds out of her bag and set it on the bed. Just like in Paris, the two of them stood in silence for a moment as they stared down at it.

"Oh, this is nuts." Pauline said as she grabbed the box and opened it. She took out the bag and emptied the contents on the bed. The pile of diamonds looked even more ominous to them now. They both swallowed.

"What have we stepped into this time?" Katherine asked. "We need to get rid of these, turn them in, and report this."

"Turn them in? Report? To whom?" Pauline exploded in frustration. "The police here in Amsterdam? This happened to us in Paris," she said as she swept her arm across the pile. "Is this something for Interpol? What is Interpol and how do we contact them? The man said this was for the 'exchange'. The exchange of what? Stolen art, drugs, weapons, sex?"

She shook her head trying to get herself under control "Look . . . until we can figure out what this is all about and exactly who we should report this to, we're going to keep these diamonds. Think of it this way," she said now that she was on a roll. "If the diamonds are for something bad, keeping them wouldn't be like we were keeping them from a charity or something?

"Pauline!" Katherine stood with her mouth open looking at her friend. "What are you saying? Where would we keep them? I'd be a nervous wreck carrying them around in my bag all day long. And, no way could we leave them here in the hotel room?"

"Hmmm." Pauline stood up and walked to the window. "You're right. We can't leave them here." She looked out at the houseboats along the canal. Then she turned, stared back at the diamonds and became lost in thought. A small smile formed on her face.

"I've got an idea." She headed back to the bed and sat down. She scooped up a handful of the diamonds, and began dropping the stones into four separate piles. "You have two and I have two. That makes four," she said over and over while dropping a stone dramatically on each pile.

"Four what?" Katherine couldn't understand what had gotten into her friend.

"Four boobs, Silly" Pauline answered. "We're going to stuff these babies in our bras." She stopped and wiggled her eyebrows. "Look, at our age, we're hanging so low that once we shove them down in there, there's no way these puppies going to fall out," she smirked.

Katherine burst out laughing and gave her friend a hug. "I love it. Let's do it." She picked up a handful of the diamonds and began sorting. "I was going to suggest we go down to the restaurant and have a cup of coffee. But, after this, I think we need to go down and have a stiff drink."

When they were done dividing the diamonds, Pauline looked at the four piles on the bed. "I don't think this is going to work. There are too many diamonds. Each pile must have over 50 diamonds," she said as she gathered up one pile and let the stones cascade through her fingers. "We'll never be able to stuff all of these into our bras. There simply isn't enough room."

"You're right," Katherine said. "But, now what do we do? I hate carrying these things around in my purse."

"Okay. Here's the deal," Pauline said. "We're going to go down to the dress shop and buy bras with larger cup sizes. That should do the trick." She looked up at Katherine for her response.

Katherine began scooping up the diamonds and putting them back into the black bag. "No way are we going to let these diamonds sit here while we go downstairs." When she was through, she put the bag in her purse, and slung it over her shoulder. Once again, she tucked her arm tightly against the purse and marched to the door. Then she opened it a crack and peeked out into the hall.

Pauline rolled her eyes as she watched her friend do her CIA act. "Would you quit acting like that? You look like a ham actor in a B-movie." Katherine made a face at her friend before she stepped into the hall.

After they purchased the larger cup sized bras, they returned to their room, sorted the diamonds in four piles again, and stuffed them in. Once they were dressed again, they examined each other.

"Good grief," Katherine said when she looked at Pauline and then down at her boobs. "We look like Dolly Parton's sisters."

Pauline laughed at Katherine's description. "Let's go get that drink now. Lord knows I need it."

"I've got good news and bad news for you about the two women," Helmut said when Dimitri arrived at his apartment shortly after he had dropped Ivan's mother and aunt off at the train station. "What do you want first?"

"Give me the good news. I need it." Dimitri said.

"Well, I found the two ladies for you," Helmut said He was still typing something into the computer. "Their names are Katherine Wilson and Pauline Maddich. They had train tickets in the same compartment as Ivan's mother and aunt. And, they even checked into the George Cinq, if you can believe that. The bad news is, they checked out early this morning. It will take me some time to find out where they are now. I'm trying to get into their credit card accounts. That should give us a trail to follow."

"Now, for the bad news, if you want me to find where the agent is holed up, you are going to have to make a phone call to him. That way I can begin tracing the call. It may take two or three phone calls to pinpoint his exact location. Does he usually stay in the same place? That would give me a good start," Helmut said.

"I don't know where he stays. This is the first time we've worked with him. But, he gave me his new cell phone number when he called me." Dimitri said and pulled out his phone.

"No problem, Dimitri. We'll find him," Helmut smiled and he turned back to his computer.

CHAPTER 13

They spent their first day in Amsterdam walking through the city. The day was perfect – bright sunshine and temperatures in the high sixties. The biggest problem walking around Amsterdam was the bicycles. Everyone rode bicycles from little children all the way up to very old people. The city even had parking lots specifically for bikes. And, the lots were crammed.

They ate lunch in a small café they had past earlier that morning. Now it was filled with the locals, so they knew the food would be good. And, it was. In the early afternoon, they took a river cruise along one of the many canals. They sat back and enjoyed the architecture of the city. It was unique and pure Dutch. The rows of narrow buildings lined the streets each topped with individual pointed roofs. Very economical and frugal, just like the Dutch personality. Nothing was ostentatious in this country. The riverboat guide told them that here in Holland only the king or queen received a salary. All the other royals had to get a job.

After the cruise, they went back to their hotel to freshen up and get a cup of coffee while planning their evening.

They were seated at a table in the hotel café. Pauline was just going to take a bite of her pastry when she noticed what Katherine was doing. "Would you stop fiddling with your boob. People are starting to look at us. You make us look like two old perverts, for crying out loud," she hissed.

"I can't help it," Katherine said taking her hand off her boob. But she still wasn't comfortable, so she rolled her shoulder and sort of leaned to the right. Then she rubbed her upper arm along the side of her breast. "There's one diamond in there that's poking me. It's been driving me nuts all afternoon." She tried to smoosh it to a better position.

"Well, just stop it. You look like a human contortionist leaning sideways like that. And, I think it would be better if we didn't use the word diamond anymore. When we're out in public, let's just call them stones, okay?"

Katherine glared at Pauline as she scrunched farther down to the right and moved her upper arm across the front of her boob. That seemed to do the trick. She sat back in a normal position.

Pauline reached into her purse. She pulled out a box of pre-filled syringes of Epinephrine called Epipens and set it on the table. "Now, listen, kiddo. I want to go over what you need to do if I get stung by a bee. There are so many flowers in bloom in this city, it's making me nervous when we walk around outside."

"Ick, Pauline."

"I know. But, in all likelihood if I do get stung, I should have enough time to give myself the shot. Once stung, anaphylaxis doesn't happen immediately. Still you've got to at least help me get the Epipen out and ready, because if I don't give myself the shot in time, I could start going into anaphylactic shock, and then I'll really be in trouble. I've told you all this before, Katherine."

"I know, but why couldn't I have been the nurse like you? Then this would be a piece of cake. We didn't have *giving shot* classes in the English department." When she saw the look on her friends face, she smiled as she reached over and squeezed her hand. "Don't worry. I'll do it. I would never let anything happen to you." She sat up straight and folded her arms on the table and became all business. "Okay. Now if worse comes to worst, tell me again how I actually give you the shot."

"All right," Pauline said. "Actually, these Epipens are really easy to use. You won't have to worry about dosage, but I do want to show you what you'll need to do to get it ready for me." She pulled one of the pens out of the box. "The first thing you have to do is get the pen out of the plastic holder. Just flip this cap off the top of the holder and slide the pen out, make sure you don't touch this orange tip, because that's where the needle is located. You don't want to end up giving yourself the shot. If you do that, we'll both be in trouble."

"Hold the pen like this and flip the blue top off. Now it's already to use. If I can't do it, you'll need to jamb the orange tip of the pen into the side of my thigh and hold it for at least ten seconds. That will push the needle out and release the Epinephrine. And, don't worry about my clothes. The Epipen is designed to go through clothing. Remember we practiced this last year?"

"I remember," Katherine said with a grimace on her face. "I'll do it. No problem there. However, I do reserve the right to whine if I have to give you a shot."

Pauline rolled her eyes and put the box back in her purse. "Nothing may happen, but I just want to be prepared. Being stung by a bee is no laughing matter. And, hopefully, if I am stung, I'll have time to give myself the shot if you get it ready for me."

Just then their waiter approached to give them a refill on their coffee. He was the same person who had waited on them at breakfast. His name was Karl and he was in his early twenties.

"How are you ladies doing?" he asked as he poured more coffee in Katherine's cup. "Did you have a nice day visiting our city today?"

"We did," answered Pauline.

"Hey, Karl. Tell us about the coffee shops here in Amsterdam. Can you really get drugs in those places?" Katherine asked.

He smiled. "Yes, you can and it's perfectly legal to do so. Would you like to go to one? I can take you if you want."

"Really!" Katherine said.

"No thank you, Karl. I don't think that's a place for us," Pauline added quickly as she shook her head and squinted her eyes at Katherine. "Don't even think about it. It's dumb," she whispered.

"Come on, Pauline. We've never done drugs because we were too old to be a part of the hippy era. Like Karl said, it's legal here. It's not like we'll get arrested. Personally, I want to see what the big deal is all about." She nodded her head as she waited for her friend's response.

Pauline turned to Karl. "You say you personally will take us to one of these coffee shops?"

"Of course. I wouldn't let you two go alone. It's not dangerous, but it would be better if you had an escort. I get off at four o'clock this afternoon. Meet me outside of the hotel. The one I am thinking of taking you to isn't far. We can walk there. And, late afternoon is a good time to go – for beginners," he smiled.

"What type of drugs do people get in these places?" Pauline asked skeptically.

"No hard drugs. The Dutch government allows only soft drugs like cannabis, what you Americans call marijuana, to be sold. You can smoke it, drink it or eat it. For you ladies, I recommend, you smoke it. Dutch cannabis is stronger than cannabis from other countries. Smoking it is the mildest way to experience it. And, here's something that will surprise you, along with cannabis, you can also order juices, milkshakes, and food in the shop I will be taking you to. So, are you two up for this?" Karl asked.

"I don't know," Pauline said slowly.

"Yes, we'll meet you outside in . . . one hour," Katherine said checking her watch.

"Got them," Helmut smiled as he sat in front of his computer. "The two women are in Amsterdam staying at the Lloyd Amsterdam. They rented a car yesterday morning and still have it. Interesting . . . they each had a charge on their credit cards at a jewelry store in Antwerp. They also went on a canal boat tour today."

"Very good, Helmut," Dimitri said. "Is it possible for you to get pictures of the two women? I think I will drive up to Amsterdam later this afternoon. At least knowing what they look like will help me when I get there. Also, keep track of their movements. Can you get me a reservation at the Lloyd Amsterdam?"

"The hotel reservation will be no problem, but getting into the system to view their passport pictures may take a day or two," Helmet said. "I can get you the make and model of the car they have rented. That should help."

"All right, anything you can provide will be a help. We have got to get those diamonds back so keep working on the women. I will call you from the road to see if you have more information for me," Dimitri said.

Helmet turned back to his keyboard. "So, the agent was taken care of then?"

"Yes, we got him early this morning when he came out of his hotel. The guy actually thought he was going to meet us to get the weapons. Idiot. Well, as least Ivan will be happy now," Dimitri replied.

The phone rang in Tony Cappelli's office. "Tony? This is Henri over at Interpol. Thought you would want to know. An arms dealer from Africa was found shot to death early this morning outside of a hotel on the west side of the city. We are trying to reach out to our snitches to see if this is related to Borovsky. I think it is."

"I agree with you. His mother comes in one day then turns around and goes back to London the next morning. Now an agent is killed. What the hell is going on here?" Tony responded. "I'll see what I can find out on my end and let you know what I hear. Keep me posted and thanks, Henri."

CHAPTER 14

When Karl left work that evening, he saw the two ladies already waiting for him in front of the hotel. Another night of free drugs, he smiled. Shortly after he got his job as a waiter, he worked out an agreement with the owner of the coffee shop. He would get free drugs each time he brought in hotel guests. So this wasn't the first time he had taken guests to the shop. However this was the first time he would be taking guests who were so old. He made up his mind that he wouldn't just drop them off like he normally did. He would stay with these two tonight. He doubted they knew the first thing about what they were going to experience, and he felt responsible for them.

The three of them entered the shop and were seated in a separate room. "So, Karl, you're telling me those traffic signs we saw on the streets that say

"*Blowverbod*" mean no smoking drugs while driving?" Katherine asked.

"Yes. Our smoking laws are quite strict in Holland. Also, that is why we are sitting here in a separate, smoking room in order to smoke cannabis. All coffee shops have a separate room for the smokers."

Karl handed each of the ladies a joint. "So, are you ready?" he smiled. He lit his own joint first, inhaled slowly, held it in his lungs for a few seconds before he exhaled. Then reached across the table to light theirs.

Pauline hesitated. "I don't know if I can do this."

"Oh, come on," Katherine said in exasperation. "We aren't going to know what this is like until we try." She leaned over for a light. She sucked on the joint and immediately started to cough. "Yuck! This is awful."

"First of all, you don't smoke cannabis like a normal cigarette. You don't need to inhale quite so much," Karl said taking a drag on his joint, holding it for a moment and then blowing it out. "See. Like that."

"All right, I'll do it," Pauline said holding the joint up for a light. But, she too took too big a drag and started coughing. "You're right, it's awful. This tastes like cow manure," she said with a pained expression on her face.

The two of them tried several more times before they got the hang of it and could inhale and exhale smoothly.

"Do you feel anything?" Katherine asked Pauline. "So far nothing for me."

"Nope. Nothing," Pauline answered blowing the smoke out slowly. "So what's the big deal?"

"Relax. Just be patient, ladies. It takes about two or three minutes," Karl said. "You will see. Pretty soon you will be feeling very mellow."

Katherine looked through the window into the next room. "Oh, look. There's a policeman, Pauline. Wave to him," she said as she waved. "You see it's legal. He's not here to arrest us, and he looks like a mellow fellow." For some reason she started to giggle.

"Actually, the Amsterdam police visit coffee shops as part of their daily routine making sure things stay calm," Karl said.

Pauline spotted him too. "He looks like a mellow fellow who doesn't bellow," she laughed with her hand flapping in the air in a wave.

Katherine burst into laughter at her friend. "That was so stupid. But, for some reason it's so funny."

Karl realized the drugs were beginning to take effect. "Now, ladies, I want to give you some instructions. Be sure to drink water when you go back to your hotel room."

"Check. Drink water," Katherine said smiling.

"Don't drink any coffee or you will get a bad headache. And, tomorrow eat a big breakfast with meat and fruit. That should make you feel better."

"Breakfast with meat and fruit," Pauline said making an imaginary check marks with her cigarette. This doesn't taste so bad anymore. Have you noticed that?"

The two of them took another drag on their joints. "Smooth. Very smooth," Katherine replied while holding the joint between her lips. They broke out in laughter again.

Karl continued with his instructions. "Don't plan on doing any serious sightseeing tonight, but tomorrow you should be feeling just fine again."

"I couldn't sightsee right now, because I think I've lost my legs," Katherine said looking under the table. She turned to Pauline. "Do you know where my legs went? How can I walk back to the hotel? I think you're going to have to call me a cab."

Pauline started to giggle. "Okay . . ." she said slowly.

"Don't you dare, Pauline. Don't you dare say it," Katherine said between snickers.

"Okay. You're a cab," Pauline finished the punch line of the old joke. Both broke out in hardy guffaws as Karl looked perplexed.

"Oh, dear." Katherine wiped the tears from her eyes. When she noticed the concerned look on Karl's face, she added, "That's an old vaudeville joke. A guys rushes up to a man on the street and says, 'Hey, buddy. Call me a cab.' And, the man says, 'Okay. You're a cab.'" They immediately broke out in laughter again. This time even Karl laughed at the joke.

When they had smoked the joints down to less than an inch and could barely hold on to them to smoke, Karl put his out in the ashtray. "I think that's all the cannabis you two should have tonight."

They slowly nodded their heads in agreement. "No, more cannabis for you," Pauline said as she gently squished the joint in the ashtray while moving her head back and forth. She put the smoked joint in the coin purse she retrieved from her shoulder bag. "We've got to save these as a memento." she said as she held the coin purse open for Katherine's used butt. "No one back home is going to ever believe this happened unless we show them our joints."

Karl reached into his pocket for some money. "Before we leave, I am going to get each of you a bottle of water. Start drinking it tonight. It will help wash the effects of the drug out of your system."

Katherine reached into her purse and gave Karl ten Euros. "No. Here. Let me get that. And, get one for yourself too." Watching Karl walk away, she leaned over to Pauline and spoke out the side of her mouth. "We have our assets covered." She waited a beat and then added, "So to speak." She and Pauline burst into raucous laughter. Each of them understood Katherine was referring to the diamonds in their bras as the assets being covered not the cost for the bottles of water.

The three of them left the coffee shop carrying their water. They took sips as they walked. Karl was kind enough to walk them back to the hotel.

"Oh, look, Pauline. There's a lamppost, but the light isn't on." Katherine seemed perplexed as she stopped and studied it.

"You dumb bunny. It's not on, because the sun is still shinning," Pauline said between meaningless giggles. Then she stopped in front of a flower display. "Aw, isn't that a beautiful tulip?"

As the three of them were admiring the flower, Karl said, "That is a toooo . . . lip." The three of them went into spasms of laughter.

Pauline spotted a bakery a few doors down. "I need something to eat. I'm famished. Let's stop in there."

"Do you suppose the bakery has potato chips?" Katherine asked. "I don't know. For some reason I can't stop thinking about potato chips."

After studying the display of bakery goods, the two women decided a mix of a dozen pastries would do the trick. They told the woman behind the counter to give them one to eat now and just add it to their bill.

The woman looked at the two as they took enormous bites of their chocolate confection. Then she asked Karl in Dutch, "Coffee shop?"

"Ja," Karl replied.

Between the bakery and the final four blocks to the hotel, the three of them managed to polish off the entire bag of pastries. Karl walked them to the elevator before saying goodnight. He hoped they would make it the rest of the way safely.

"At least this wasn't like drinking too much," Pauline said after they entered their room. "We were able to walk back here without reeling down the street like we would have had we been drunk."

"Yeah. Cannabis just makes you feel kind of slow," Katherine said as she sat down on the bed and took a big swig of her water. She set the bottle on the nightstand and lay back on the bed.

After Pauline took off her coat and hung it up, she turned to her friend. Katherine was sound to sleep. She was laying on her back with her arms outstretched. Her legs were dangling over the side of the bed. She was still wearing all her clothes including her shoes and spring coat. "Oh, boy," Pauline muttered as she lifted Katherine's legs up onto the bed. She was dead weight. "Well, no way am I going to try to get you undressed. You can sleep in your clothes. It serves you right for talking us into doing this dumb thing tonight," she whispered.

Then she sat on the side of her bed and also took a sip of her water. I'm going to lie here a minute before getting undressed, she thought. That was the last thought Pauline had before she too drifted off.

CHAPTER 15

When Katherine woke, she realized she was very, very uncomfortable. She seemed to be lying on lumps and she was unable to wiggle her toes. She was disoriented for a moment when she opened her eyes. What am I doing on top of the covers with all my clothes on including my coat? And, why am I still wearing my shoes? How did that happen? Oh, good grief, the marijuana. I must have fallen asleep as soon as we came back last night, she thought. She sat up and looked across at the other bed. Pauline was also lying there on top of the blankets with all her clothes still on. She shook her head smiling as she stood up. Then out of the corner of her eye, she saw herself in the mirror.

"O-M-G," she whispered as she slowly approached it. Her hair was sticking up and down and out. Yikes. This is beyond a bad hair day. My clothes are so rumpled. I look like a bag lady. And, what's that brown stuff on my face, she thought as she leaned in closer. It looks like chocolate. Ugh, must be from those pastries we ate last night.

She turned and took a better look at her friend. "Pauline, are you awake?" she asked. Yup, Pauline looks as scary as I do, she thought. She walked to the bed and shook her friend. "Pauline," she said softly again.

Pauline opened her eyes and shouted, "Oh, my God!" when she saw what Katherine looked like standing there.

"Yeah, that was my thought too. Come on you have to see this." She went back to the mirror and motioned for her friend to join her.

The two of them stood looking at themselves. They both started to laugh. "So this is what two seventy-one year old junkies look like." Pauline took a whiff of her sleeve. "And, why do I smell like a skunk?"

Katherine went to get her phone and brought Pauline's back too. "Listen, we have to take a pictures of this. We're going to have everyone in stitches back home when we show them what we looked like the morning after smoking only one joint of cannabis." They stood, arms around each other and took pictures of their reflection in the mirror.

Katherine said, "You know we should send these pictures to our kids. Wouldn't that give them a heart attack?"

After they finished taking pictures, they showered to get rid of the *skunky* smell from their previous night's adventure. When they stuffed the diamonds back into their bras and finished dressing, they started down to breakfast.

"Make sure none of those diamonds are poking you," Pauline said when they were on the elevator. "I don't want you groping yourself at the table again."

Katherine gave a pursed lip look at her friend before she moved her shoulders around and flexed her arms. "Nope. Everything is comfy. I'm good to go," she responded just as the door opened.

They entered the dining room and took a seat near the entrance. Katherine looked at the menu. "Remember, Karl told us to eat a big breakfast." Then she added, "You know I don't feel the effects of that reefer at all. How about you?"

Pauline just shook her head. "Reefer?" she chuckled. "One joint and you think you can talk like a junkie? You make me laugh, you old fool."

Katherine smiled and wiggled her eyebrows. "Who ever thought we would be smoking our first joint when we were seventy-one years old? Now that was the kind of adventure I was talking about having."

Katherine checked out the menu and decided on bacon and eggs. "So what do you think we should do today? I'd like to visit the Rijks Museum. It has a Vermeer Exhibition I'd like to check out."

"Okay. Sounds good," Pauline said.

Dimitri had arrived at the hotel late the previous evening and was now seated at a table in the corner of the hotel dining room. He was about to order breakfast. Helmut still hadn't sent him pictures of the two American women. But, when the two older women entered the room a moment ago and sat down at a table near the far wall, he decided to keep an eye on them because they looked American and seemed to be the right age.

He wanted to find out if they were the ones he was looking for, so when his waiter came to pour his coffee, he asked, "See those two women sitting over there near the entrance? I think I know the woman in the green jacket. Is she Italian? Would you happen to know if her name is Maria?"

Karl was the gentleman's waiter this morning. "No. Her name isn't Maria. It is Katherine. As far as I know she isn't Italian either. She and her friend, Pauline, are from America. And, they are very nice ladies," he added with a smile.

"Ah," Dimitri said. "Well, I guess I was mistaken then."

Hah, got you, Katherine and Pauline. This was easier then I thought it would be. Now what to do? Do I wait to see if they leave the hotel and then search their room for the diamonds or do I follow them to see if they have the diamonds on them? Helmut said they had credit card charges when they stopped in Antwerp, so in all probability they must realize what they have are diamonds. And, chances are high they would not leave them sitting in a hotel room. I think following those two and trying to get them alone somewhere would be better.

CHAPTER 16

Rather than drive to the Museum and waste time trying to find a parking place, the women took a cab. It let them off close to the entrance. They were surprised to learn places in Holland, like the Museum, didn't offer Senior Citizens discounts on the tickets. The discounts were for children and students. Somewhat disgruntled they paid full price to get in and began their exploration.

"Oh, I could stand in front of this Vermeer all day," Katherine said looking at the portrait of the woman pouring milk. "See how he plays with the light. Your eye is drawn to the milk the woman is pouring. I really would like to see the "Girl with the Pearl Earring". But, that's hanging in the museum in The Hague."

"I like this painting too," Pauline said as she studied it. "But, what really floors me about all of these Dutch

Masters is how they were able to capture the beauty and delicacy of the lace on the women's dresses, and the fact that we can stand so close to the paintings. Unbelievable. Good choice to come here, Katherine."

The Rijks Museum was huge. It would require a full day or more to be able to see all of the exhibits. After three hours they decided to leave, because it was a beautiful day in Amsterdam. Tulips were in bloom everywhere. It was perfect for strolling before they went for lunch.

Rather than return to the main entrance, they exited through a side door and walked along the back of the building. They only needed to make one more turn around the building in order to reach the walkway ahead that led down to the canal. It was a weekday and not many tourists were in the city yet. It was quiet. The sounds of the street were muffled on this side of the building. It was just the two of them as they strolled along making their plans for the rest of their trip.

Dimitri had been following the women all morning. He gave them a few seconds before he too left the building by the side door. Once outside he realized this area was isolated. He knew it would be his best chance to confront the two of them, so he increased his pace.

"So, where do you want to go next?" Pauline asked. "Should we go up and visit the Scandinavian countries? Personally, I would like to go south and drive along the Mediterranean Sea. Maybe start in Italy and go west through Provence along the Sea to Spain."

"Would you mind making one stop on the way? One place I have wanted to visit again is Austria," Katherine said. "I've particularly wanted to go back to Vienna and Salzburg. If we do that then we could shoot down to Slovenia before going over to Italy. So let's go south and leave the Scandinavian countries as our last stop before we head for home."

Pauline switched sides so she wouldn't be walking next to the flowers. "Should we keep the rental car or turn it in and start traveling by train?"

"I think we should . . ." Katherine started to answer her friend when a man behind them said, "Good afternoon ladies. Are you enjoying the day?"

Both of them were somewhat taken aback. They hadn't realized anyone was there. Katherine saw that the man looked like a businessman. He was dressed in a well-cut blue suit. The blue and red, stripped tie stood out against his white shirt. He was rather tall, about six feet. There were flecks of gray in his dark hair. He appeared to be somewhere in his forties. And, he smelled good.

That's some mighty expensive cologne he's wearing, she thought.

"Ah . . . yes this is a nice day," Pauline said as she and Katherine kept walking. The man came along side of them as they made the turn around the backside of the building. Now they were really alone. Not another person in sight, and there were no windows on this part of the building either. Unconsciously, the two women moved closer to each other.

"Did you enjoy the Museum?" he asked pleasantly.

Katherine looked at Pauline questioningly. "We did," she answered slowly. The man said nothing. More to break the silence then out of curiosity, she asked, "Were you touring the Museum?"

"Actually, I was in the Museum, but I didn't see many of the exhibits, because I was following you two."

Both women were stunned. "What?" Katherine stopped and confronted the man. "What do you mean you were following us?"

"Well, Katherine, I have been following you and Pauline, because I know you have the diamonds and I want them back. Where are they?" He turned his hands out, cocked his head and shrugged his shoulders in a silent questioning gesture.

"Oh, brother," Pauline muttered.

"How do you know our names," Katherine asked without thinking, but then added quickly, "If those really are our names."

The man smiled like a fox cornering a baby rabbit. "I know all about the two of you," he said slowly. "You were given a box of diamonds by mistake at the café in Paris. They belong to me. And now, I want them back."

"What? When? Paris? We haven't been to Paris," Pauline responded. "Diamonds? What the heck are you talking about? Diamonds," she said with a snort.

Because the two of them had been friends for so many years, Katherine immediately picked up on what Pauline was doing. "Yeah, we don't have any diamonds," Katherine joined in with bravado.

"Ladies, ladies, ladies," Dimitri said as he slowly shook his head at them. He reached into the inside of his jacket and pulled out a gun. "Now . . . Give me those diamonds."

Katherine and Pauline instinctively gave a small yelp before grabbing each other.

"A gun?" Katherine said in a raised voice. "I've never had anyone point a gun at me in my entire life!"

"Dear, God." Pauline said still clinging to her friend. "Why do you think we know anything about diamonds?"

"Because I know the man we were doing business with gave you the diamonds when you were at the café in Paris. He's dead, by the way. He made a mistake and thought you were someone else. I know you have them. Why else did you make a stop in Antwerp to visit a jeweler?"

Katherine took in a breath of air, but at that moment a bee started flying behind the man. Pauline zeroed in on it. The man continued speaking to them. Something about the George Cinq and the Eurostar, but she was so concentrated on the bee that his words weren't sinking in.

"Ah, sir . . ." she said as she pointed a finger at it.

"Don't move," Dimitri said forcefully swinging the gun in Pauline's direction. Keeping his eyes focused on the women, he merely swatted the air near his head as the bee flew closer.

"Oooh. Don't do that!" Pauline said with a grimace. Ugh, that guy is loaded down with cologne. No wonder he's attracting the bee, she thought.

The bee came back at him again. Again, he swatted it without taking his eyes off the women. But, the third time the bee came back with a vengeance and stung him right on the side of his neck.

Pauline cringed. She knew it hurt. Dimitri slapped his neck and yelled a word in Russian.

I don't know what he just said, Pauline thought. But, I am willing to bet that was a beauty of a curse word.

Dimitri shrugged his shoulders and moved his head around without taking his eyes off the women. The gun in his hand never wavered. The look on his face turned ugly. "Enough, ladies. I am done. You will give me the diamonds or so help me I will shoot you right here. Then I will find the diamonds myself," he said glaring at them.

"Oh, oh," Pauline whispered as she watched drops of sweat began to form on the man's forehead.

Oh, oh is right," Katherine said not taking her eyes off the gun in the man's hand. "Looks like we need to just give him the diamonds."

"No. That's not what I meant. I think the guy's going into anaphylactic shock." Pauline watched him shake his head as if he were trying to clear it. His hand holding the gun started to shake. He was having trouble breathing. Then, he clutched his throat with his free hand. The gun dropped from his other hand and he slowly sank to his knees.

By now Katherine had her mouth open as she stared at the man. "What's happening, Pauline?"

"It's the bee sting. He's going into shock."

"That's what happens in anaphylactic shock?" Katherine asked incredulously watching the man crumble. "That's what would happen to you if you were stung?"

"That's it," Pauline responded.

Slumped on the ground the man was now making gargling noises.

"Let's get out of here," Katherine said frantically tugging on Pauline's arm.

"I can't," Pauline said slowly shaking her head. "I can't leave him here like this. He'll die." She looked at her friend and quietly shook her head in resignation. She swung her purse off her shoulder and reached in for her kit of medicine.

Pauline went to the man and bent down next to him. "Go get help, Katherine. I'm going to give him a shot of my Epinephrine."

She was so focused on what was going on with her "patient", she never noticed Katherine bend down and pick up the man's gun. After Katherine put it in her purse, she started down the path to get help.

The man was still conscious but was really having difficulty breathing. There was fear in his eyes as he fought for each breath. Pauline went into her nurse's mode and started working quickly. She laid a hand on his arm for reassurance. She couldn't remember all the times her patients told her how much her touch meant to them.

"I'm a nurse," she said looking into his eyes. "I'm going to help you."

"Arrrg" was the man's only response.

She set the Epinephrine kit on the ground. "Has this happened to you before?" she asked.

"Naaaa," the man shook his head terrified.

"Don't worry." She squeezed his arm. "I'm going to give you some medicine that will make you feel better."

As she prepared the Epipen, she kept up her banter. "This is called an Epipen. One of the nice things about it is I can give you the shot through your clothing. That makes this much easier. I am going to give you the shot in your leg." She gave him a calm smile.

Again she put her hand on the man's arm for reassurance. "Okay, here we go. You should begin to feel the effects of the medicine very soon," she said and plunged the needle and released the Epinephrine into his thigh.

After a few moments the terrified look began to ebb from his face. And, his breathing seemed to be getting easier. Pauline smiled at him all the while holding on to his arm. "You're getting some color back in your face. Is the breathing getting better?"

"Yes," Dimitri said in a whisper.

"Okay, now we need to get that stinger out of your neck. That's very important."

She used a piece of tissue from her purse to protect herself from any of the bee's remaining venom. With it wrapped around her fingers, she grabbed the tip of the stinger still lodged in the side of his neck and slowly pulled until it came out. "Ah, there we go. Got it," she smiled at him.

"My friend went to get help. You need to go to the hospital to be monitored. This isn't over."

"No" Dimitri shook his head. "No." He started getting a frantic look on his face.

"Hey. You need to calm down. This one shot isn't enough. You could still go back into shock again. You need to be watched for the next few hours." Just then she heard Katherine coming back.

"Pauline," Katherine called out as she rounded the corner. "I brought the Museum guard with me. How is he doing?"

She dropped to her knees next to Pauline. "Oh, wow. You look a lot better," she said to the man.

Pauline turned and looked up at the guard. "Do you speak English?"

"Yes. What is the problem?" he asked.

Thank goodness, she thought. I don't have to waste time with a language barrier.

"I'm a nurse. You need to call for an ambulance. This man was stung by a bee and went into anaphylactic shock. I have the same problem, so I carry Epinephrine with me at all times. I just gave him one of my shots and he seems to have some relief. But, it is important that he go to the hospital to be monitored."

The guard took out his walkie-talkie and stepped away to relay the message for an ambulance.

Dimitri tried to rise. He was agitated. "No, no hospital."

"Sir," Pauline said as she put her hands on his shoulders and tried to keep him lying down. "You don't have a choice. You must go."

"Wait a minute. I think I know what the problem is." Katherine leaned close to the man's face. "You don't have to worry," she whispered to him. "You can go to the hospital. They aren't going to find your gun. I took it." She gave him a wink as she patted his cheek.

"What?" He jerked up and tired to grab her arm.

"What?" Pauline hissed in sotto voce. "Are you crazy? What did you do with it?" Her eyes were almost squinted shut. She had been through so many escapades with Katherine, she was afraid to hear the answer.

Katherine leaned toward her friend and whispered out of the side of her mouth. "Not to worry. It's safe. I have it in my purse."

"What have you done?" Pauline said in an angry whisper.

Katherine looked hurt. "Hey, I was thinking of you, kiddo. I didn't know if this guy would come around and be able to use it while I was getting help."

Dimitri had a hold of her arm. "Give it back," he said through clenched teeth.

"Shhh. The guard's coming back," said Katherine trying to pull her arm out of the man's grip.

The guard reattached the walkie-talkie to his belt. "The ambulance is on its way. Is there anything I can do while we are waiting?"

Pauline opened her purse and took out a pad of paper and a pen. "Actually, I'm going to give you a note explaining what I have done for this man." She wrote down the name and dosage of the Epinephrine shot.

"Here." She tore it off and handed it to the guard. "You need to give this to the medics when they arrive.

Tell them to be sure to give it to the people at the hospital. They will need to know this information."

After a few minutes they could hear sirens in the background. Pauline had the man in a sitting position by the time the medics arrived. He still protested going to the hospital. But when he started to have difficulty breathing again, he gave up the fight and agreed to go. He gave Katherine a murderous look as the medics came with the stretcher.

One good thing about being in Europe, unlike the United States, there wasn't a mountain of paper work that needed to be filled out. The guard wrote down their names and where they were staying for his report then he told them they were free to go. They couldn't get back to their hotel fast enough.

CHAPTER 17

"Katherine Wilson and Pauline Maddich," Tony Cappelli said when the two names popped up on the Embassy computer screen. Per the Eurostar train manafest the Embassy technician had just pulled up, the names of the two women who had tickets in the same compartment as Borovsky's mother and aunt appeared on the screen.

The computer search for the women began, because his friend, Henri, from Interpol called earlier this morning.

"Listen, Tony. Would you mind going into your Embassy computer and checking on train tickets for the Eurostar? See if there were also two women who had tickets in the same car or compartment? Your computer is much faster than the one I have access to here at the police station."

He told Tony his snitches confirmed the dead man was definitely here from Africa to purchase arms from Borovsky. But instead of giving the diamonds to

Borovsky's mother and aunt, he made a mistake. He gave the diamonds to the wrong women thinking they were Borovsky's mother and aunt.

"Apparently, the idiot followed the two women all the way from London thinking he was following Borovsky's mother and aunt," Henri told him. "Remember when I told you about Ivan's mother complaining about a missed train on the phone call outside of the George Cinq? I think the guy picked up those other women when they got on the train in London thinking they were Borovsky women. And, somehow they either sat in the seats or near the Borovsky seats. And, I have a feeling following Borovsky's mother rather than giving the diamonds to the wrong women is what got him killed."

"Also according to my sources," Henri added. "Borovsky sent his henchman, Dimitri Zarenko, to find those women and get the diamonds back. Let me know if they are from Europe. For their safety I need to get to them before Zarenko does."

"No problem," Tony had answered.

That's why he was now sitting next to the Embassy's computer technician as he checked the Eurostar ticket information. It was confirmed. Katherine Wilson and Pauline Maddich had tickets in the same four-seat compartment as the Borovsky ladies.

Tony asked the technician to do one more search. "Henri wants to know if we can find out what country the women are from. If they're from somewhere in Europe, as a member of Interpol, he is responsible and needs to track them down."

The technician was studying the names of the women. "See anything interesting about those names?" he asked Tony.

"No. What about them?" Tony asked.

"Different countries," the technician said and pointed to the computer screen. "One woman is named Wilson and the other Maddich. If they are from Europe, chances are they would both have a last name from the same country rather than one with an English name and the other with a Slavic name like these two have. I'm going to check the U.S. Passport data base first and see what happens."

Sure enough, Katherine Wilson and Pauline Maddich were U.S. citizens who entered Europe through England two weeks ago. The tech then pulled up copies of the actual Passports. They were both seventy-one years old, about the same age as Borovsky's mother and aunt. Both had their place of birth listed as Wisconsin.

"Well, it looks like this is one for us then. As U.S. citizens, we're the ones who need to protect them," Tony said. He looked up at the technician. "Can we find out where they are now? See if they're still at the Cinq. If not, find out where they are and what they've been doing. I've got to make some phone calls." He got up to return to his desk. When he had taken two steps, he stopped.

"Hold it. Wisconsin – the Midwest. The flat-vowel ladies! Son-of-a-bitch." Tony turned back to the technician. "About four days ago, I think I was standing right in front of these two women while I was waiting to cross the street. Then later that same day I saw them again in the Cinq. What were they saying at that intersection?" He began to pace back and forth.

"I was paying attention to their accents more than their words. But, you should have heard them, pure Midwest." He smiled briefly at that memory.

"Come on, come on, Cappelli. Think. What were the words? Something about a box – *is it heavy*, one of them asked. I remember that. And, one used the word *weird*. Weird what?"

He hurried back to his desk. First, he had to call Henri. As U.S. citizens, it now became his responsibility to keep them safe from Zarenko. And second, to do it, he needed as much information about these two women as he could get.

CHAPTER 18

As soon as the two women got back to their hotel, they quickly packed their suitcases and checked out. Pauline felt it wouldn't be long before the man was released from the hospital. And given what happened earlier this afternoon, she was sure he would come after them again as soon as he got out, especially since Katherine took his gun. She still couldn't believe her friend did that.

They were in the car and Pauline was driving. She hadn't even given Katherine a chance to offer to drive out of Amsterdam. When the valet brought their car to them, she just took the keys and got in the driver's seat. They entered Germany a half hour ago and were driving along the Rhine River. Neither had done much talking. Both were still trying to process what happened to them.

Katherine was looking out the window. They were traveling through farm country. The landscape was dotted with widely spaced farmhouses and barns. "Pauline?" she said softly.

"What?" Pauline asked.

"Why didn't we turn that man in to the police when we had the chance?"

Pauline was surprised by her friend's question. "I . . . I don't know," she answered slowly and rather bewildered. "I guess I was so busy treating him as a patient, I wasn't thinking straight. He really would have died if I hadn't helped him, you know?" She nodded her head as if trying to confirm her reasoning. "When you went to get help, did you think of finding a policeman?" She looked over at her friend.

"No," Katherine said with a helpless gesture. "I was so stunned at what happens when a person goes into anaphylactic shock. The only thing I could think of was to get help and get back to you as quickly as I could. I was afraid a bee would sting you and I wouldn't be there to help you."

They became quiet again. After some time past, Katherine broke the silence and said, "See if you can find somewhere isolated to pull off the road. We need to stop and take a moment to calm down. And, I think we need to take a look at this gun," she added slowly.

"Ugh, that horrible gun. You never should have taken it, Katherine," Pauline said disgustedly.

"I know, but at the time, I couldn't leave you alone with that man and this gun laying there. I'm not the one who's a nurse. I didn't know anything about anaphylaxis. I didn't know if he would be able to get his hands on the gun again while I was gone."

"I know. I know. I'm sorry. I shouldn't be yelling at you. Thank you," she said as she reached over and took Katherine's hand. "But, honest to goodness, the idea we have a gun scares me."

Katherine squeezed Pauline's hand. "That's why we need to stop and be still for a while. No driving, no nothing. Look's like you can take any of these exits, then drive in a ways and look for a quiet spot."

Pauline took the next exit and went north. Then she turned off the main road onto a side road and drove about a quarter of a mile before stopping on the soft shoulder. They got out of the car and walked a short way into a field. There were no other people around. It was late afternoon. The sun was low in the horizon. It really was quiet as they listened to the birds in the trees.

Katherine took the gun out of her purse and examined it. It was sleek, made out of some sort of black metal and quite heavy. "Sure doesn't look like the six-shooter Hopalong Cassidy used to use, does it?" she said. Since she had never handled a gun before, she had no way of knowing whether it was loaded or not. Her first thought was to turn the gun and look down the barrel to see if she could see bullets. Fortunately, the word "dumb" popped into her brain before she did that.

"I'm going to pull the trigger," she told Pauline. "I want to know if it's loaded. And, I want to see what shooting a gun is all about." She held the gun out in front of her aiming toward the open field.

"Wait a minute, Katherine," Pauline said holding up her hands and taking a step back. "I don't think that's a good idea. You don't know anything about guns."

Katherine lowered the gun. "What's to know? You pull the trigger and a bullet comes out. Right? Besides, there's no one around." She brought the gun back up. "This is a perfect place to do it," she said right before she squeezed the trigger.

Kapow! Zing! Crack!

The gun flew out of her hand, because she wasn't prepared for the kickback when she fired it. "Yikes!" she yelled.

Down in the field, a small branch of a tree fell off. Leaves gently wafted to the ground. About twenty birds flew out of the tree squawking loudly.

"Good Lord, I didn't know that would happen," she said looking at the gun on the ground. "And, it's so loud. I didn't think it would be that loud."

"Oh, my god. Oh, my god," Pauline shouted. She began prancing up and down like a New York City Rockette.

Katherine turned and watched her friend bouncing around. "Oh, for crying out loud, Pauline. You look like the Drum Major for the University of Wisconsin marching band."

"Don't you dare," Pauline yelled back. She was so angry. "Don't you dare make fun of me. I'm scared. Someone threatened to kill us today, for God's sake. We just snuck out of the second city in four days." She held up four fingers and shook her hand at her friend. "I'm hungry. We haven't eaten since breakfast. And, what about these, huh?" she asked cupping her boobs and hiking them up. "We've got over a million dollars in diamonds shoved in our bras. We look like Wagnerian sopranos on steroids for crying out loud!"

"Shit," she yelled.

Whaa?" Katherine stood with her mouth open and gaped at her friend. In all the years she had known Pauline, never once had she ever heard her utter one swear word.

"Shit, Katherine," Pauline yelled even louder. Her hands were balled into fists. "You idiot. Don't you realize you could have killed us with that gun?

The trigger could have snagged on something in your purse and it could have gone off in the car."

"Ka-ka-poo-poo. Shit!" she screamed at the heavens.

Katherine stood there stunned. The entire day flashed before her eyes.

The stress of fleeing a city because some wacko threatened us with a gun, then actually stealing the gun . . . what was I thinking? My best friend is flipping out shouting words I've never heard her use before. And, those damn birds are still squawking overhead.

There was nothing left for her to do. She tilted her head back and started to laugh uproariously.

By now Pauline was taking in gulps of air trying not to cry. She looked over at Katherine who was doubled over with laughter. Between deep sobs and sucking in air, what they had been through and the absurdity of her reaction to it, hit her. She gave one last cry of anguish before she too joined in the laughter.

Once they had both gotten control of themselves, they ended up hugging each other.

Katherine stood back with her hands on Pauline's shoulders. "Aw, come on, Kiddo," she said as she gave her friend a slight shake. "Good grief, think about it. You and I have been through so much in our lives and we always got through it. We're going to get through this too. Whatever the hell *this* is." It was more of question then a statement.

Katherine picked up the gun and examined it one more time. "I'm quite sure all guns have safeties on them so they can't go off accidently. Ah . . .this looks like it." She pushed a lever on the side of the gun. "Now don't go ballistic on me. But, I'm going to shoot this gun again to make sure that really was the safety I just pushed." She held the gun out in front of her, turned her head to the side, scrunched her eyes shut and tried to pull the trigger. It didn't work. She opened her eyes and looked at the gun. "Okay. It's off." She gingerly put the gun back into her purse.

"Now, we need to find a place to stay for the night. And, we need to get something to eat. So let's quit this fooling around," Katherine said with a wink as she took her friend by the hand and led her toward the car. "Give me the keys. I'm driving. You need to sit back and relax for a while."

After she opened the door to the driver's side, Katherine stood and looked at Pauline over the top of the car. "By the way, where did you ever come up with something as lame as *Ka-ka-poo-poo?*" she asked.

"Yeah, that," Pauline said sheepishly while she opened the passenger door and got in. As Katherine was putting the key into the ignition Pauline said, "Last month my four-year old grandson threw a hissy-fit and said that. It was the only thing I could think of on the spur of the moment. She shook her head and chuckled. "But it sure relieved the stress."

"Well, Pauline, the important thing is, for the first time you ever said a swear word, you gave it your best shot." Katherine smiled and chucked Pauline on the arm. She turned the key and started the car.

After making a u-turn, they traveled back to the main road. Shortly before they reached the on-ramp to the Autobahn, Pauline said, "We need to talk about what we're going to do about all this. The gun, the diamonds." She cocked her head and gave a slight chuckle, "Our lives."

"I know. But, not now," Katherine responded. "After we're settled in and fed, we'll talk about it. So be quiet and just enjoy the scenery." She smiled and reached over and patted her friend's arm.

CHAPTER 19

Ivan was getting very upset. The idea his dear mother had been followed all the way from her home in London, no less, was unnerving him. He was having trouble sleeping. He couldn't think about anything else. The fact he hadn't heard from Dimitri for two days only added to his agitation.

"So, did you find the women and get the diamonds back? Why have you not called me?" Ivan asked frantically when Dimitri finally phoned him.

"I could not call you, Ivan, because I was in the hospital. But, I did locate the women," Dimitri said. "They were in Amsterdam."

"Hospital? What are you talking about *hospital?*" Ivan demanded.

"That is what I am trying to explain. I had them. But then I got stung by a bee and went into – what is the word? Ah yes . . . anaphylactic shock."

"What the hell are you saying? Anafatic shock? A little tiny bee made you go to the hospital. What type of lies are you telling me?" Ivan was starting to lose his temper. "So no women, no diamonds? Nothing, but lies? Is that it, Dimitri?"

"Ivan, calm down. I am telling you the truth. I located the women in Amsterdam and while I was talking to them, a bee stung me. And, I almost died. That is the truth, Ivan. Pauline, one of the women, was a nurse. She gave me a shot of medicine that saved my life. Then I went to the hospital and had to have another shot." Dimitri knew he was sounding crazier by the minute to Ivan.

"I am out eight hundred thousand Euros. That is what I believe. This is your fault. You did this to me. You stabbed me in the back. Stung by a bee! What horseshit. I will not tolerate betrayal. And, you have betrayed me, Dimitri." Ivan came out of his chair and began pacing as he shouted into the phone.

"I will give you one more chance to find those women and get my diamonds back. And, when you find the women, kill them. I want them dead. They are the ones who caused all this. They are the ones who caused my mother to miss her train. They took the diamonds delib-erately. And, if you do not do this, I will find them and you and kill all of you myself. All of you will be dead. Do you hear me?" Ivan was so out of control, spit began drooling from the side of his mouth as he screamed.

Dimitri had never heard Ivan talk so crazy before. He was sounding paranoid. Learning his mother was followed seemed to have pushed him over the edge.

"Ivan, calm down. Listen to me. Those women did not cause your mother to miss the train. You know that. It just happened. The two American women had train tickets in the same compartment as your mother. It was the idiot agent who thought they were your mother and aunt. And, he has been taken care of. Now let me explain . . ."

"Americans!" Ivan spat. "How do you know the women were Americans?" he asked.

Dimitri groaned silently. He knew Ivan was going to really explode with this piece of news. "I used Helmut and his computer to track the women."

"Helmut," Ivan roared. "You went to that Kraut and told him my business when I specifically ordered you not to involve anyone else in this? I told you this was to be just between you and me. If you were here right now, I would shoot you, Dimitri. You disobeyed my orders."

Dimitri was getting headache again. "Ivan, please. Calm down. I know how upset you are about your mother being followed. I have taken care of that. Now I am going to get the diamonds back for you." But without any more killing, he thought. No way will I kill Pauline. She saved my life. She could have left me there, but she didn't. She stayed and gave me her own medicine. And, Katherine could have brought the police back when she went for help, but instead she only brought the guard. Neither of those women deserved to die. The only thing I might do is smack Katherine around for taking my gun. He sneered to himself.

"No," Ivan said. "I am coming to Amsterdam. When you go to get the diamonds I want to be there with you. I want to look those women in the eye. I want them to see they cannot trick Ivan Borovsky and not pay for what they did to my mother. And, if you lose them again, you are a dead man, Dimitri," Ivan warned him.

"The women are no longer in Amsterdam. They left the city when I was in the hospital." Dimitri held the phone from his ear, because he knew what was coming.

"Traitor!" Ivan screamed. "You are nothing but a traitor. You let them get away from you and then you make up this lie about being in the hospital. You no longer work for me. You are fired, Dimitri. Fired, I tell you. I will find them myself. I will get the diamonds back myself. They will pay for what they did to my mother and so will you!" He slammed the phone down so hard the receiver broke into pieces.

Dimitri slowly disconnected the call. It is over, he thought. He knew for certain that Ivan was no longer mentally stable. His fixation with his mother was always unhealthy, but his reaction to this was beyond unhealthy. It was frightening. He needed to find the women fast. They did not deserve what Ivan would do to them if he got to them first.

CHAPTER 20

Katherine and Pauline had driven as far as Koblenz, Germany located along the Rhine River when they stopped for the night. They were able to enjoy their first meal since breakfast in Amsterdam.

Pure bliss shone on Katherine's face when she finished the last forkful of spaetzles and knackwurst. "Oh, that was good." She looked over at Pauline. "Okay, now let's talk about what we're going to do."

Pauline took a sip of coffee. She didn't set it down, but held the cup in her hands as she was thinking. "Well . . . the first thing we need to do is to get rid of these diamonds." She nodded at Katherine's boobs. "We can't keep running around putting our lives in danger like this. But, the question is who do we give them to? I've been thinking," she said slowly. "I have no idea about the police system here in Europe. I don't think the local police would be much help in keeping us safe after we turned over the diamonds. I've heard about Interpol, but what is Interpol? What does it do and more importantly where the heck is it? So I think our best bet is to go to an American Embassy and ask for help. What do you think?" She set the cup down and looked questioningly at Katherine.

"I agree. There was nothing funny about that man pulling a gun on us today. And as Americans, I think the Embassy will be our best bet at keeping us safe too." Katherine stared straight ahead and seemed lost in her thoughts. "Let's plan on going to the Embassy in Vienna. That's got to be a major one, and easy to find. They should be able to help us."

"But here's the deal, Katherine. We can't walk up to the Embassy carrying the gun. Even though I'm quite sure the United States is the only country on the planet stupid enough to have next to nothing gun laws, they are not going to let us get one inch inside the front door while we're carrying a gun," she snorted. And I bet walking around any of these countries here in Europe with a loaded gun is against the law, period."

"My friend, Judy, at the condo, has a daughter who works at the U.S. Embassy in Rome. She said her daughter told her when an American breaks the law in a foreign country, there is very little the Embassy can do. The person must serve the imposed sentence when they do something dumb. So we need to figure out how we can ditch the gun now without getting caught. And . . . we need to ditch it where no other person can find it. I don't ever want anyone else getting their hands on it and be able to use it. That would be horrible"

Katherine nodded in agreement. "Yeah, you're right. I agree. To be honest, I've been thinking the same thing ever since I fired it. Holy cow, I couldn't believe how loud it was." Katherine started to chuckle. "I was just thinking about those crazy squawking birds that came out of the tree."

Pauline groaned.

"Okay, okay. I'll stop," Katherine said. "Now let's figure out a good place to dispose of it. What if we throw it in the Rhine? It should sink to the bottom. We'll throw it as far out into the middle as we can, so it'll be next to impossible to find. We'll walk down there tonight and toss it in. Then we'll be done with it."

"Good. Let's go down about eight o'clock. It should be dark enough by then. No one should see us throwing it in." Pauline picked up the dessert menu. She was still hungry and they had about an hour to kill before it was eight o'clock. Eating a German pastry was better than sitting in their hotel room chewing their nails until it was time to go, she thought.

"What is with these people? Don't they ever go to bed?" Katherine asked in exasperation as she stood on the walkway along the Rhine. They had been walking up and down the esplanade for the past forty-five minutes trying to find a lonely spot. But, every time they thought no one was around and she prepared to get the gun out of her purse, someone in the distance would begin to approach and she had to stop. They hadn't had more than ten or twenty seconds without walkers, runners or bicyclists going by.

"Forget it. This isn't going to work," Pauline said. "We're never going to find a spot without people near us. We'll look for somewhere to dump it while we're traveling tomorrow. It's getting late. I don't think it's safe for us to be walking around too much longer anyway."

"Well, if we are accosted, we can just pull the gun out and scare the crap out of the mugger." Katherine smirked. When Pauline didn't respond to her joke, she shrugged and said, "Well, enough of the comedy for tonight." She put her arm through Pauline's. "Come on, we'll worry about getting rid of this thing in the morning."

Back at the hotel, the two checked their email messages before going to bed. Pauline switched over to her browser to check the map of the area and asked, "Have you ever been to Switzerland?"

"No," Katherine responded. "Out of all the countries John and I visited, that was one we never made it to. What about you and Frank? Did you guys go there?"

"Nope, we never made it to Switzerland either. I'm looking at the map of the route from here to Vienna. You know, we could take a slight detour to the west and be in Zurich well before noon tomorrow. It's not that much out of our way. And, maybe while we're in the mountains, we could see if we can get rid of the gun. Want to do Zurich?" She looked over at Katherine.

"Yeah. I'd like that. How long would it take? What time would we have to leave tomorrow morning?" Katherine asked.

Just then her cell phone rang. Katherine looked at the caller ID. "It's Priscilla. Oh, boy. I bet she's calling to carp about that morning-after picture of you and me in Amsterdam," she chuckled.

"Hi, honey. How are you?" She waited for the blow up from her daughter while making a face at Pauline.

"Mother? Are you okay? Where are you? The FBI are here and they say you're involved in a Russian arms deal."

"What?" Whatever Katherine expected to hear, this wasn't it.

"What have you done? What have you gotten yourself into this time? Oh, Mother, how could you?" Priscilla wailed.

"Wait a minute. Wait a minute. What are you talking about? Russian arms deal? You say the FBI told you Pauline and I are involved in a Russian arms deal? Are the FBI there now?" Katherine pushed speaker on her phone and covered the phone with her hand.

"You've got to hear this," she whispered to Pauline. "Apparently, the FBI thinks we're mixed up in a Russian arms deal. They're at Priscilla's house right now."

"You're kidding." Pauline was dumbfounded. "See, I told you those diamonds were for something bad."

"Diamonds? What diamonds. Mother, what's going on?" Priscilla screeched.

"Rats, she heard you," Katherine whispered to Pauline.

Just then Pauline's phone rang. "Oh, brother. Now it's my son." To avoid static with Katherine's phone, she walked across the room to answer it.

"Hello, Dennis. How are you, Honey?"

"What the hell is going on, Mom? The FBI are at my house and the agent says you're a Russian arms dealer."

"You've got to hear this, Katherine. The FBI is at Dennis's house too," Pauline whispered as she put her phone on speaker.

"Now, Dennis, don't get excited. Katherine and I have everything under control. And we are not arms dealers."

"What do you mean under control? Every time you get with that crazy Katherine, she manages to get you in trouble," Dennis roared.

"Hey, I heard that Dennis," Priscilla yelled through her phone. "Don't you dare call my mother crazy. Your mother is just as nuts as my mother. It's the two of them together that causes all the trouble."

"Who the hell is that? It sounds like Priscilla. Is she there with you?" Dennis asked.

"No, she's not here, Dennis. She's talking to Katherine and we put you both on speakerphone. So, it might be a good idea to keep your voice down," Pauline said.

"The hell with that," he roared again. "You went running off to Europe without telling us you were going. Now I have FBI agents in my house asking about you. I've had it, Mom. You get yourself home right now. You're going to stop this foolishness."

Pauline's head popped up. She pursed her lips together just before her eyes became tiny slits. "Now you listen to me, Dennis. Don't you even think about ordering me around, because I've had it with you always telling me what to do! Katherine and I have been walking around with over a million dollars in diamonds trying to figure out how to get rid of them. This morning, we took a gun away from a man who was threatening us. And now we can't figure out how to get rid of that either. And, and . . . I smoked pot. Hah. Whadda ya think of that? So don't you try to tell me what to do." She nodded her head for emphasis.

"Way to go, Pauline," Katherine said as she smiled at her friend across the room. "About time."

"Gun?" Priscilla shouted from three thousand miles away. Katherine winced. She could hear Jane bawling in the background. It figures, she thought.

"Mrs. Wilson, this is Agent Harder. I'm here with your daughters, Priscilla and Jane. Can you tell me how you got the diamonds your friend mentioned. And, am I correct, you ladies have a gun? Where are you now, Ma'am?"

Pauline looked over at Katherine and grimaced. "What the heck is going on?" she asked quietly. "This is nuts."

"Hey, wait a minute . . ." Katherine said slowly to the agent. "Why are you asking us all these questions? How do we even know you're from the FBI? How do we know the guy in Amsterdam didn't send you to our children's homes? Put my daughter back on the phone. I want to be sure she's all right."

"Ma'am, I am Agent Harder and I am with the FBI. We got a request from the American Embassy in Paris to locate you and see if you need any help."

"Oh, yeah? Paris, huh. Why would the Embassy in Paris call you? We haven't been in Paris for over a week. How would they even know who we are?" Katherine persisted.

"Sir, give me the phone," a voice said in the background of Pauline's phone. "Hello, Mrs. Maddich? This is Agent Brown of the FBI. Are you and your friend okay? Where are you, Ma'am? We can send someone to help you if you're in trouble."

"Thank you," Pauline answered. "But, we don't need any help. Besides we're leaving for Zurich tomorrow morning anyway. And, then we are going to the

American Embassy in Vienna to turn in the diamonds and the gun."

Katherine seemed frantic. She waved her hands at Pauline to get her attention. "I just thought of something," she whispered. But, she forgot to hold her hand over the phone, and everyone heard her. "We need to hang up right now. You know how, McGee, on the T.V. show, *NCIS*, is always able to trace where the bad guys are through their cell phones? Hang up and shut your phone off, Pauline, so these guys can't get a bead on us," she said as she ended her call.

"Ma'am, do not hang up," Agent Brown said to Pauline right before she too ended her call.

"Russian arms dealers?" Katherine said with a smirk. "How about that for adventure?"

"Good grief. Now we have to sneak out of another city. Might as well start packing," Pauline said as she went to get her suitcase.

"No. We're not leaving. We're going to stay here tonight. Then tomorrow morning we're going to have a nice breakfast before going to Zurich. We are not giving up on that city," Katherine answered with finality.

"I don't know, Katherine. I think we should just go directly to Vienna and turn these diamonds in," Pauline said pointing to her boobs. "This is not an adventure. This is turning into a nightmare."

"Nuts to people chasing us. Nuts to being afraid. Now I'm just mad. We're staying put. We came here for a vacation, damn it. And, that's what we're going to do. Go to bed. We'll talk in the morning." Katherine gathered her pajamas and cosmetic kit and stalked into the bathroom.

CHAPTER 21

The next morning in Paris, Tony Cappelli called his friend, Henri, at Interpol. "Henri, can you come to the Embassy this morning? During the night, I received a cable from our FBI agents in the United States. It pertains to the two women involved with Borovsky. The cable was waiting for me when I came in this morning. I requested the FBI contact the Wilson and Maddich children in the States. I'm going to need your help. And, per the cable, the two ladies definitely have the diamonds, and, you're not going to believe this, somehow they got a hold of a gun."

"I can confirm the diamonds," Henri said. "Once you gave me the names of the women, I pulled up a report from a jeweler in Antwerp who was suspicious of those very same women when they came into his store last week and had two diamonds appraised."

An hour later, the two men were sitting at Tony's desk. He pulled out the cable and began to shake his head. "Wait until you hear this FBI report," he chuckled. "These two ladies seem to have had quite a time. They just left their third city in four days. We're using electronic surveillance now to keep an eye on their car as they're traveling. They told the agents they were on their way to Zurich. So we started scanning the roads from Koblenz to Zurich trying to locate them. We picked them up twenty miles outside of Koblenz this morning. And, right now, it looks like they still are headed for Zurich."

"So, why do you need me?" Henri asked.

"Well that's just it. The FBI said the women told them they have a gun. They also told the FBI they had plans to go the American Embassy, but in Vienna. They didn't explain why they want to stop in Zurich first. But in any case with Borovsky involved, I don't want to wait until Vienna. I want to reach them before that, and that's where I need your help. Can you contact the Zurich police and ask them to detain the women until I can get over there and get them? And I'm going to need you with me when I go, just in case the local police have a problem and want to charge them with gun possession."

"How did those two get a gun?" Henri asked incredulously.

"I'm not sure, but I think they took it from Dimitri Zarenko when they were helping him in Amsterdam," Tony smiled. "The Dutch authorities sent our Embassy a copy of an incident report involving two American women. It states that Katherine Wilson and Pauline Maddich gave medical aid to Dimitri Zarenko who had been stung by a bee and had an allergic reaction. As I understand it, Pauline Maddich is a nurse. Apparently, she gave Zarenko a shot of something that saved his life. He was taken to the hospital, but there was no mention of a gun found on him. So if he had one, I think they took it."

"That sounds unbelievable. Zarenko, the one everyone fears, gets his gun taken away by two little old ladies." Henri started to laugh. "Some days this job can be fun."

"Well, it gets even funnier," Tony said holding up the cable. "Both of the FBI Agents said they thought the two women could be dangerous, not because they're professionals, but because they sounded like two, and I am quoting, 'fruitcakes'."

"Fruitcakes? What does that mean?" Henri asked.

"It's an American idiom. It means someone who is crazy or eccentric," Tony smiled. "The Agents think if the two women do have a gun, they may be dumb enough to try to use it and in the process either get themselves or others killed. According to their children, neither of them has ever handled a gun."

Just then an Embassy secretary entered Tony's office. "Excuse me, but Mr. LeFlore has an urgent phone call from Interpol. Would you like me to transfer the call to your phone?" she asked.

"Of course, put the call through, Eileen. Thank you," Tony responded. When it rang, Tony indicated that Henri should answer the call.

"Allo," Henri said in French. He listened for a moment.

"Oui," was his response. His face took on a somber look.

"Oui," he repeated after a moment. His brow furrowed and his eyes squinted. He looked like he was in pain.

"Oui," was his answer again.

This time he shook his head slowly. "Sacre bleu," he said quietly.

"Oui, oui. Merci," he said before hanging up the phone.

He looked across the desk at Tony. "That was Zarenko," Henri said.

"Zarenko? He's contacting you? Is he working for you?" Tony asked.

"No. He is not one of ours. But he knows me by reputation. He figured once we found the dead arms buyer, we would start putting two and two together. His call pretty much confirms what we know about the ladies. They were on the train from London. The buyer mistook them for Borovsky's mother and aunt and gave them the diamonds. Dimitri has been tracking the women. He cornered them in Amsterdam. But when he got stung by the bee and went to the hospital, they took off." Henri rolled his eyes and shook his head at that one.

"The problem is Borovsky has gone off the deep end. He fired Zarenko, because he thinks he is a traitor. Dimitri said he has never heard Ivan talk so crazy. Now Borovsky thinks the two women deliberately sabotaged his mother and aunt causing them to miss their train in London. He's positive the women did that so they could steal the diamonds. Ivan is trying to find them himself and kill them. Dimitri received a text message from their computer guy. Borovsky apparently kidnapped the guy and is keeping him with him at all times to help track the women. Right now, Ivan is on his way to Zurich. Dimitri is going to try to reach the women before Ivan does."

Tony ran a hand over his face. "Holy shit. Those two women don't know how dangerous this has become. We need to get to Zurich as soon as possible."

"I will call the police there and tell them we are coming. We have got to get those women to safety," Henri said while he took out his cell phone and began looking up the number of the Zurich Police Department.

CHAPTER 22

The drive to Zurich took less than three hours, which was perfect, since it would allow the two friends time to check out the city after they got settled in at the Bed & Breakfast.

Pauline took in sights of the city as Katherine drove. "Oh, Katherine. This is one of the most beautiful cities I've ever visited." She couldn't seem to turn her head fast enough to take it all in. "Lake Zurich, the mountains in the background and the magnificent architecture. Wow!"

They were stopped at a stoplight, so Katherine finally had a chance to look out the window at their surroundings. "I'm so glad you suggested making this detour. It's just what we needed after the past few days."

The light turned green and Katherine proceeded through the intersection. "I can't wait until we stop and

I have time to really see this city too. It's not easy driving and trying to see the sights at the same time," Katherine added as she turned down the street along the river. "Okay, per the instructions from the Bed and Breakfast person we talked to this morning, there should be a parking structure on the next block. There it is on the right."

They entered the structure and found a parking place on the second floor. They got their luggage out and went to the elevator. It was a six-block walk to the B & B, but it was such a sunny, beautiful day that walking would be a pleasure for them.

Pauline pressed the button. Stepping into the elevator, she said, "As soon as we check in, let's arrange a tour of the city. I don't want to miss a thing while we're here."

The quaint B & B was located down a narrow street in a small building that must have been at least two hundred years old. The lobby was decorated with Swiss antiques. There were several clocks ticking away on the walls around the room, delicate lace doilies dotted the tables, and small toys were artfully displayed in curio cabinets.

"Good morning, ladies," the young girl at the desk smiled. She looked as if she was about nineteen or twenty years old. "Welcome."

"Oh, this is just lovely," said Katherine as she approached the desk. Pauline stopped at the kiosk to look at the tourism brochures. She gathered the ones that looked interesting before coming to the desk herself.

"Checking in will be a little slow this morning. I do apologize for the inconvenience. Our computer went down early this morning. So I must do your check-in by hand," the young girl told Katherine when she laid her passport and credit card on the desk. "I will only be able to scan a copy of your passport and credit card. I will then enter the information as soon as our computer is back on-line. The repairperson should be arriving shortly. Again, I do apologize for the inconvenience."

"That's no problem for us. While you're scanning our documents, it will give us more time to look at the beautiful items in your lobby. Besides, years ago there were no computers. Everything was done by hand. We're used to it." Katherine smiled at the girl trying to ease her embarrassment.

Once they were checked in and settled, the two women left the B & B to explore. They spent the next four hours on a bus tour of the enchanting city taking notes of places they wanted to revisit tomorrow. They decided to leave their car in the parking structure and either walk or take taxis while in the city. On the recommendation of the young girl at the B & B, that night they ate at a restaurant where the locals ate. It was less than a mile away, so they took a leisurely stroll to the bistro.

"This is a lot like German food, but not so heavy. And I am definitely saving room for dessert. I want something made with Swiss chocolate tonight." Pauline wiggled her eyebrows at her friend.

Katherine smiled as she looked at the dessert menu. "Let's order two different desserts and then share them. So, what do you want to do tomorrow? I suggest we just enjoy the day. No tours, no lectures, no guides. I'd like to do some shopping while we're here too. Some of the shops we saw from the bus this morning looked very interesting. You know, this seems like the first time we've been able to take a breath of air in days and act like real tourists. It seems safe here."

"Katherine, what have we gotten ourselves into?" Pauline asked seriously. "Russian arms dealers, for god sake. And, that damn gun. We still have to get rid of it."

"Whoa, two swear words in three days, you wanton woman, you," Katherine chuckled. "Listen, I've been thinking . . ."

"When you do your thinking, that's when we get into trouble." Pauline looked pained.

"No, listen." Katherine put her arms on the table and leaned closer to her friend. "When we leave Zurich for Vienna, I want to go up into the Alps. I love the mountains. So, let's ask our girl at the B & B if she knows where we can ride a cable car. When we get to the top, we'll stay awhile. We'll walk around and look for a path into the surrounding woods. Once we find a lonely spot, we'll toss the gun away. If there is still snow on the ground up there, all the better to ditch it."

Pauline shrugged. "Okay. I can't think of anything better to do."

When the bill came, they paid it using Euros. They each brought five hundred Euros to Europe with them, but because their lives had turned upside down in Paris and they spent the last week sneaking in and out of city after city, they hadn't had a chance to spend any of them.

This morning before they left Koblenz, Katherine declared that that was it. "We need to calm down and start acting like tourists. In a few days we'll be in Vienna and our problems will be over. We're in no hurry. So get your Euros out." Other than gas this morning, they hadn't charged anything all day.

On their walk back to the B & B, they stopped at a candy store and bought chocolate. "Just in case we get a craving during the night," was Pauline's justification for the purchase.

"Where the hell are those two old ladies?" Tony Cappelli yelled in frustration while looking at the street monitors in the Zurich Police Headquarters. He and Henri had flown in an hour ago and had been electronically following the women's car on the highway as they reached the outskirts of Zurich. But, when the women entered city, some of the monitors were down and they lost them.

"Jeez, billions of dollars of electronic gear and we can't even keep track of two grandmothers, for God's sake. Have you got anything on their credit cards?" he asked the police technician at the computer across the room.

"No, nothing, so far. Are you sure these ladies came to Zurich?" the man asked.

Tony shot him a murderous look. "They're here. We saw them enter the city, until your cheap equipment broke down."

"Hey, Tony. Calm down," Henri said putting his arm around Tony's shoulder and giving him a slight shake. "We are going to find them. And, we are going to do it before Borovsky does."

Tony took in a deep breath of air and let it out slowly. He turned back to the technician and shook his head. "I'm sorry. I didn't mean that. We have been tracking these women for days now. And, every time we get close, things go wrong. I shouldn't have taken this out on you."

The technician just shrugged as if dealing with rude, impatient Americans usually ended up like this. "I'm going to start checking the hotels," the technician said. "Hotels have to register their guests with passport information. If you say they are grandmothers, I do not think they will be sleeping on a park bench," he added with a smirk. Tony stifled a sneer as he looked at the smart-ass technician.

By eleven o'clock that evening, they had done all they could. They hadn't found any trace of their car; no indication they checked into a hotel; and, no credit card activity. The policemen on all the shifts had received pictures of the two women. The officers who walked their beat showed their pictures in the various tourist places. No one remembered seeing them. The street monitors that weren't broken were being monitored, but still no sign of the women or their car. It was Henri who suggested they finally call it a day and get some sleep. He and Tony decided to return to the Police Headquarters at seven-thirty in the morning.

CHAPTER 23

The next morning while they ate breakfast, Katherine and Pauline decided to check with their young friend at the front desk of the B & B to see if she could suggest where they could go for a cable car ride up into the Alps tomorrow on their way to Vienna. Hopefully, it would be somewhere convenient and not too much out of the way. Both of them were anxious to get rid of the gun and get to Vienna and be rid of the diamonds.

"Oh, I see your computer is working again," Pauline said when she neared the front desk.

The girl had a frazzled look as she worked to catch up on the data entry. But, she stopped and smiled at them. "Good morning to you ladies. Yes, as you can see the problem was finally resolved late yesterday afternoon. Now I am trying to get caught up with all the entry work. I am hoping to be done before I leave today."

She pushed enter on the computer and then gave them her undivided attention. "Now how may I help you two?"

"Tomorrow we're leaving to drive over to Vienna. But, before we leave Switzerland, we would like to take a cable car ride up into the Alps. Where can we go to do that?" asked Pauline.

"Hmm. You say you are on your way to Vienna?" the girl asked. Katherine and Pauline nodded their heads. She reached under the counter and brought out a map. She unfolded it and said, "I have just the place for you to go. I hope you do not think me presumptuous, but my cousin runs a cable car business in the Alps." She smiled sheepishly. "It is in Lichtenstein. However, it is not out of your way at all. I will show you."

She turned the map around for the women and retrieved a yellow highlighter from the cup next to her computer. "You can leave Zurich in the morning along this route," she said and began marking the route. "You can be there in less than two hours. Even if my cousin did not own this business, I must tell you the scenery and the view from up there is beautiful. You will not be disappointed. You will be able to see the Alps in all their splendor."

"Then you see," she said as she continued to highlight routes on the map, "you can continue on to Austria through the mountains here. Or, you can take this road north out of the mountains and continue east here. Unless you really enjoy driving through nothing but mountains for a very long time, I would suggest you travel north and continue your trip in the lower country." She refolded the map and handed it to Pauline.

"Thank you so much. This is just perfect. And, I like your suggestion of driving out of the mountains too." Pauline put the map in her purse and then turned to Katherine. "Ready to go?"

Before the women walked away, the girl winked. "Mention my name to my cousin. Tell him I said to give you a discount. His name is Wilhelm." The two ladies laughed as they walked out the door.

They spent the day leisurely enjoying the city. One of the brochures Pauline had taken yesterday morning when they checked in was a map of city. They used it to locate an upscale shopping district. They had such fun just browsing through the various stores. Fortunately for their pocketbooks, neither of them had an overwhelming urge to buy anything. Zurich attracted money from all over the world via the Swiss banks located throughout the city. Consequently the prices of merchandise in these types of stores were way out of their league.

In the early afternoon, they decided to take a taxi to the shores of Lake Zurich and have lunch at an outdoor café.

"This is just beautiful," Katherine said looking out at the blue of the Lake and the mountains in the background. "It's like we're sitting inside of a postcard."

They had a light lunch of small sandwiches and soup and were now enjoying the last bites of their desserts. "This is pretty spectacular, isn't it?" Pauline remarked. "I wonder if the people who live here and see this vista everyday even notice it anymore. Are they so busy going about their daily routine that all of this becomes mundane to them?" She swept her arm across the view in front of them.

They paid their bill and decided to take a stroll along the Lake before going back into the city. After a while, they sat down on one of the benches that dotted the walkway. This was one of the few times since England they even had time to be calm and do nothing. Both were lost in their thoughts as they sat quietly side by side.

"Pauline, would you ever get married again?" Katherine asked still looking out at the Lake.

Pauline wrinkled her nose before she turned to her friend with a questioning look. "Married? What the heck brought that on?"

"I don't know." Katherine shrugged her shoulders. "The scenery, the quiet, time to think. She looked back at her friend, "Well, would you?"

Pauline shook her head slowly before she answered. "I don't think so. I'm too old. It would be nice to share my life with someone again though. But, at our age the only thing we would share would be our aches and pains and keeping track of each other's medication. I've been a nurse. I don't care to go back to that. I wouldn't mind dating again. But, even that gets complicated. About a year ago, I went out with Jim Lucca a few times." Pauline looked out at the Lake as she said this.

"Eey-yoo. Jim Lucca? We went to high school with him. He always thought he was so hot. I thought he was just plain conceited." Katherine blew out a breath of air making a disgusted noise.

"I know, but I had a crush on him back then. He never even knew who I was. Last year his wife died and he moved into my building. When he gave me the eye-ball," Pauline gave Katherine a come hither look, "I thought why not. So what if it's fifty-five years later."

She seemed lost in thought. She looked at Katherine out of the corner of her eye and said softly, "Not only did I date him, I went to bed with him too."

Katherine's jaw dropped and her eyebrows seemed to shoot up into her hairline. Surprise and amusement flitted across her face simultaneously as she gave her friend a shove. "Get out of here, Pauline," she squealed. "Are you kidding me?" Then with a wicked smile on her face she asked, "So how was it?"

Pauline had a slight smile on her lips. "Well, it was slower than I remembered it. But it's like riding a bicycle. Once you learn how, you never forget. It wasn't bad. And, it was nice to have someone hold me again. You know, whenever we were out, Frank always held my hand." Pauline paused and then added softly, "I miss that closeness."

Katherine gave Pauline the quiet time to think about her husband, Frank, that she seemed to need. But, finally she couldn't stand it any longer. She did not want to drop the subject, because this was just too incredible. Details. She wanted details. "Ah . . . what about the arthritis in your hip?" Didn't that sort of, I don't know, change the rules?"

"Well, that's just it. I never even thought about my hip while we were in the middle of doing the deed," began Pauline.

"Doing the deed," Katherine interjected with a chuckle.

"But, the next day, my hip was killing me so badly I had to take pain pills all day!" Pauline laughed.

Katherine laughed out loud too. "So are you still dating him?"

"No. The dumb cluck. The next time we had a date, he showed up at my door with his shaving kit and toothbrush asking if he could keep them in my condo. As if one time meant entitlement," she sneered.

"I told you he was conceited," Katherine nodded her head up and down for emphasis.

"How shallow can you get?" Pauline agreed. "And guess what? By the end of the week, he was already seeing another woman in our building. Per the gossip, she puts out." She made a disgusted face and rolled her eyes.

After a pause, Pauline raised her chin and looked at Katherine with slanted eyes. "Okay. I've bared my soul. Now what about you? Have you dated anyone since John died?"

She shook her head and shrugged her shoulders. "No. For a while after he died, I was too busy trying to learn how to be single again. And, there were a few things I wanted to do. I went out East to visit my sister. Took a fun course at the University. Went down to Central America with Priscilla. Did some interesting things with my grandkids, like white-water rafting. Then when I got those things out of my system and turned around, I realized how old I was. Now I agree with you. I'm too old to get serious about the dating thing. And, think about it. As far as adventure or excitement goes, men our age equate getting in on the early-bird special with discovering a new species in the Amazon."

Pauline smiled at Katherine's description. "What about your friend, Arthur? You're both widowed. Why haven't you dated him?"

Katherine jerked up and stared at her friend in surprise. "Arthur? Good grief. What are you talking about? I've known him for ages," she answered waving her hand in a dismissive gesture.

Katherine became pensive and looked out at the Lake. "Why would you me ask about Arthur?" she asked quietly looking back at her friend.

Pauline got exasperated. "Oh, you are so obtuse sometimes. I've seen him look at you. He looks at you like your *lunch* for heaven's sake."

"What!"

"Lunch. Trust me."

Katherine didn't know what to say. She sat there with a bewildered look on her face. "Lunch?" she mouthed staring at Pauline questioningly. "Oh, come on. I don't believe that for a minute."

"Lunch," Pauline gave a decisive nod answering with finality.

"Huh." Katherine sat there shaking her head and went back looking out at the Lake. Pretty soon a small smile began to form at the corner of her mouth. A gleam appeared in her eye. She shook her head in a jaunty way when she turned to her friend.

"Goodness are those diamonds?" she asked in a falsetto ingénue voice. She put one hand on her hip and the other hand behind her head. Using her best Mae West impression she said, "Yah, and goodness had nothin to do with it."

Both women broke out in laughter. "What do you think? Will Arthur think I look sexy? Katherine wiggled her eyebrows.

Pauline put her arm around Katherine's shoulder. "When Mae West said that she looked sexy. You just look silly. But, oh my, fifty-five years later, you still make me laugh."

A half an hour later, they hailed a taxi and went back to the B & B. They needed to pack, since they planned to leave very early the next morning. They wanted to spend time in the mountains and still have enough time to drive out of them while it was daylight. That night they ate dinner at the B & B.

The young girl at the desk of the B & B didn't finish entering all the Passport information of the guests into her repaired computer until the end of the day. By the time the information was sent to the city Tourist Office, the clerk had already gone home for the day and wouldn't be entering that information into the Police computer system until the following morning.

CHAPTER 24

By seven o'clock the next morning, Katherine and Pauline had eaten breakfast, checked out of the B & B using their credit cards and were now on the road to the cable car company in the Alps.

By eight o'clock that morning all hell broke lose.

Once the credit card charges went through, Borovsky knew where the women were staying. Right from the beginning, he had demanded Helmut keep a constant check on the women's credit card activity. Finally after two days, charges popped up. When Helmut told him what he had found, Ivan grabbed him and made him drive to the B & B hoping to intercept the women before they left.

Fifteen minutes later, the police technician down-loaded the women's passport information sent from the Tourist Office. Actually, he hadn't planned on doing that task until later in the day. He was tired of wasting his time on two little old ladies, since no one had explained why this was so important. But when he came in this morning, the rude, impatient American wouldn't shut up until he checked the hotel guest file.

As soon as they learned where the women were, Tony and Henri sped off to the B & B with a police car following close behind. Because the B & B was located down a narrow alley-like street built hundreds of years ago, it was open to pedestrians only. They had to park their cars on a cross street and proceed the rest of the way on foot. They rushed through the ancient thoroughfare.

The young woman at the desk had a surprised look on her face when the two men and the policeman burst through the door. They produced their IDs and began to question her about the whereabouts of Katherine and Pauline.

"The women checked out early this morning right after they finished eating breakfast," she said. She looked at them questioningly as she was reaching under the counter to pull out a map. "Those women must be very important. You are the second group of policemen who came here this morning asking about them."

Tony rocked back on his heels, closed his eyes and raised his face to the ceiling. "Borovsky," he said in frustration to no one in particular.

"Mademoiselle, what did the other policemen who were here earlier look like?" Henri asked the young woman in a casual manner.

"Well, there were two of them. I think they were detectives since neither of them was wearing a uniform. One was young and he did all the talking. The older man just stood there and said nothing. But, you know? The older man scared me. And, he looked Russian too. I remember thinking how odd it was for the Zurich Police Department to have a Russian working for them."

"What time were they here?" Tony asked getting himself back under control.

"Oh, I would say about fifteen minutes ago," she responded.

"Is there any possibility you know where the two women were going when they checked out this morning?" Please say yes, Tony thought beseechingly.

"As a matter of fact I do," she smiled and held up the map. "That is why I pulled this out. I can show you exactly where they are planning to go today." She uncapped the highlighter and opened the map while she told them about her cousin's cable car company in Lichtenstein. She then highlighted their route and added the fact that after their cable car ride, the women planned to proceed to Vienna by going north out of the Alps.

"Did you give the other men a map and tell them where the women were going, Ma'am?" Tony asked quietly.

"Yes, I gave them a copy of this map also," she replied.

"Merci, Mademoiselle," Henri said. He folded the map and put it in his suit pocket. He took out his wallet. "Here is my card. Please call me if anyone else comes in here to question you about the women, whether they are policemen or not. And, ah . . . it would be a good idea not to tell them where the women have gone. N'est pas?"

She took the card from Henri and looked at it. Her eyes widen and she gasped. "Interpol! Oh, dear. Now I am frightened. What have those women done? They seemed so nice too. Did I make a mistake by telling the other gentlemen where the women have gone?" She seemed very agitated.

"No, no, no, Mademoiselle. You have nothing to be frightened about. We just need to reach them. They have an ah emergency back home in the United States. We need to inform them about it." Henri hoped his easy manner and explanation would calm the young woman.

"Thank you, Ma'am. You have been most helpful," Tony added. He nodded to Henri indicating he wanted to leave. There was nothing more to be done for the young woman. Now that Borovsky knew where the women were, they couldn't waste valuable time.

He and Henri and the policeman hurried out the door and ran back to their cars. On the way, Henri took the map out of his pocket and handed it to Tony. "Listen, Tony. You take the map and follow the women. I am going back to the police station with the officer. I will be able to check the highway monitors to see if we can spot their car. And since they are going to cross the border into Lichtenstein, I will need to alert Interpol in that country to also begin monitoring. I will be coordinating the two countries and it will be simpler to do it from the station. Be sure to keep your phone on so I can keep you updated as you drive."

"All right." Tony had his hand on the door handle when he stopped, cocked his head to the side, and looked at Henri out of the corner of his eyes. "Do you trust Zarenko?"

That question wasn't expected. It took Henri a few beats to reply. "Well, I . . . I do not know. Why are you asking?"

"I'd like you to try to contact Zarenko. See if he knows where Borovsky is right now. Tell him where the women are going and see if he can try to get to them and stop Borovsky. Those two need all the help they can get. And I guess I'm asking because if we do contact him, will he help us or will he use what we tell him to help Borovsky?"

Henri ran his hand over his face. "That is a good question. He did call me in Paris and warn me that Borovsky was after the women. That has to count for something." He looked at Tony and shrugged his shoulders. "All right. I will make the call and feel him out before I tell him what we know."

Tony unfolded the map and laid it on the roof of the car to study it. The policeman showed him directions out of the city in order to reach the route the women had taken. He blew out a large breath of air as he got into his car. He gave a short wave to Henri before he made a U-turn and drove away.

"Dimitri? This is Henri from Interpol. Are you in Zurich?"

"Hello, Henri. Yes, I am here. I assume this call is about our two American friends," Dimitri said.

"Yes. Do you know that Ivan has learned where they are and is following them this very minute?"

"What the hell? All right, Henri. Start from the beginning and tell me what is going on. I received a text from Ivan's tech kid, Helmut. He said Ivan kidnapped him and they are trying to locate the women. I have not received any messages from the kid for over twenty-four hours. To tell you the truth, I was worried Ivan had killed him. However, if they are following the women, good. The kid must still be alive and with him. No way is Ivan capable of tracking them by himself."

Henri was in a quandary. Dimitri sounded sincere, but he also knew Dimitri could be ruthless. He wasn't convinced. He would ask a few more questions before he told him anything more about the women.

"Dimitri? Why are you helping us with these women?"

"Damn if I know Henri. I will not lie to you. Getting my hands on eight hundred thousand Euros worth of diamonds would be very good. I could set myself up in business. Borovsky is done. He is not sane anymore."

Henri sucked in a breath of air when he heard that.

Dimitri gave a small laugh. "Do not worry, Henri. There is more. If Ivan reaches those women he is going to kill them. That is a certainty. *I cannot let that happen.*" He emphasized each word.

"I had a gun pointed at those two in Amsterdam. I was going to shoot them myself when that bee stung me and I went into anaphylactic shock. They could have run away. I could not have stopped them. But Pauline did not run. She sent Katherine for help. Then she stayed with me and gave me her own medicine. When the Museum guard came back with her friend, they could have told him to call the police. But Pauline told him to call for an ambulance instead. And again, she stayed with me until it came. No one has ever done anything like that for me in my entire life, Henri. I cannot let Ivan kill them."

Now Henri was sure. He could use Dimitri. "The women are on their way to Lichtenstein to ride a cable car in the Alps. Ivan is about an hour behind them. He knows exactly where they are going, because he has a map."

"Dreck! Henri, tell me how I can get to those women. If Ivan finds them, he will shoot them on sight. If anyone tries to stop him, chances are he will shoot those people too. The kid sent me a text saying Ivan walks around with his gun in his hand all day long. He's terrified. That is why I thought Ivan might have killed him already. I have to be careful replying to the kid's texts in case Ivan learns we are in communication."

Henri spent the next ten minutes laying out the route the women were taking to the cable car. Then if they managed to elude Ivan, the route they would be taking to Vienna.

CHAPTER 25

Katherine and Pauline were sitting on a fallen log looking out over the valley at the surrounding mountains in all their majesty. It was unbelievably quiet. The wind was gently blowing through the few pine trees up here. The large birds that built their nests in this altitude were silently soaring in the air. The air was crisp up here. The sky seemed to be a deeper blue than in the valleys below. The women hadn't spoken for the last few minutes. They were just enjoying the calm and peace of the place. Both had a serene look on their face as they seemed to be rejuvenated by the splendor of the Alps.

They had ridden the cable car up to the end of the tree line on the mountain. When they got off they followed a path into the sparse forest looking for a place to get rid of the gun. But they both agreed even up here someone could come upon the gun while hiking and be able to use it.

Katherine had the gun out and was examining it. "I wish we knew how to take it apart like they do in the movies. Then we could throw the pieces in different places and be done with it."

Pauline looked terrified. "Don't even think of trying to dismantle it!"

"I know. I know. I'm just thinking out loud, Pauline. I'm not stupid."

Once they made the decision to keep the gun, they continued to walk farther along the path and found the fallen log and sat down.

It was Katherine who broke the silence. "Pauline, do you ever think about dying?" Katherine asked the question while taking in the view in front of her.

Pauline didn't turn her head either. She too continued to look at the vista in front of her. "Of course. At our age how can we not. The decades of our lives are behind us. Only years are in front of us now." She looked over at Katherine. "There's a sixty year study on aging going on at the National Institutes of Health in Baltimore. They found that old people don't fear death. They accept it. I remember chuckling at that one. My first thought when I read the finding by the researchers was – for this you got a PhD? So, yeah, I have thought about it. Actually, I want to live until I am eighty."

"Really?" Katherine turned toward her friend. "I don't have a magic number to make it to. Personally, I want to go until I go in a ditch, whether that's tomorrow or next year or ten years from now. When I can't do the things I want to do, then that's it. I want it to be done."

Pauline smiled. "That sounds so like you. But, um, are you trying to tell me something? You're not sick, are you?"

Katherine sighed in exasperation. "Good heavens, no," she said firmly. "If I ever do find out I have a serious illness, you'd be the first one I would call, for heaven's sake."

She looked back at the vista before her. "I don't know . . . I was just sitting here looking at these magnificent mountains and thinking they have been around for millions of years. And, humans have such a puny average life expectancy of what? Seventy-eight point five years. Here we are on this wondrous planet and we will never have the time to see it all. Even if we travel everyday of the year, we can never see every island, every country, or every town. We're so insignificant in the scheme of things." She shrugged her shoulders in a helpless gesture with palms up. "And, then one thought led to another. That's all. Not to worry, kiddo."

Pauline took Katherine's hand and gave her friend a wink. "Just checking. I wanted to be sure." After a moment, she added, "Well, since we can't ditch the gun, I guess its time to go back down and get ourselves to Vienna."

When Helmut pulled into the cable car parking lot, Ivan scanned the lot and spotted the women's rental car. "Stop! Stop the car," he shouted. "They are here." He waved his gun at an open parking slot. "Come on. Come on. Pull in. Pull in." Before Helmut could even take the key out of the ignition, Ivan had his door open. He ran around to the driver's side and pulled Helmut out. "Hurry. I've got them now," he added with glee. Helmut had a look of pure terror on his face as Ivan grabbed his arm and dragged him to the queue for the cable cars.

Dimitri had made good time. He arrived at the parking lot shortly after Ivan. Fortunately, the police hadn't been patrolling the road. He had been able to travel well over the speed limit the entire way. He also spotted the women's car. They must still be here, he thought as he parked and got out of his car. He relaxed somewhat when he saw Ivan and Helmut just as they were about to enter the ascending cable car. There was no sign of the women near Ivan. He felt he still had time to help them. He wanted to follow Ivan. But, he stopped and stood next to his car. He didn't want to risk Ivan seeing him.

Once the cable car carrying Ivan started up the mountain, Dimitri hurried over and got in line for the next car. He could see the car he would be taking slowly coming down the mountain. At mid point, Ivan's car going up and the car he would be boarding passed each other.

Business was brisk. People were already ahead of Dimitri when he got in line. The cars were traveling so slowly. He was becoming extremely anxious as he waited for his car to arrive. He flexed his hands and shifted his weight from one foot to the other. I have to get up the mountain to stop Ivan from doing anything crazy. This seemed to be taking forever. Finally the car came around the bend, but stopped ten meters away to let the descending passengers off first. He couldn't believe the number of people the car was capable of holding. He was getting frantic now. It is taking too much time for them to depart.

Through the windows of the unloading car, he could see there were only two more people left to depart. He wanted to run down to that platform and yank them out of the car. Then he thought his heart would stop beating. The last two passengers off were Pauline and Katherine. A huge smile lit up his face. Those are two are the luckiest ladies I have ever met, he thought. They missed meeting Ivan by one cable car. In fact, their two cars just passed one another. But now I have to get off the ramp. I need to intercept those slippery ladies before they have time to take off in their car.

In order to get out of the boarding line, he had to work his way through the line of people behind him. Without causing any disruption, he courteously began moving down. He didn't want the ladies to turn around to see what the grumbling was all about. If they spotted him, they would be gone in seconds. He tried to move down the middle of the ramp while keeping them in view.

As the hide-and-seek game between Dimitri and the ladies was going one, Tony Cappelli raced into the lot. He arrived just as the two women were walking down the departure platform. "Thank God they're alive," he said out loud when he saw them. He looked around and saw their car parked near the end of a row of cars. There was an empty slot right next to it. He zoomed over and pulled in, got out and stood at the rear of his car while he waited for them to approach. He checked out the area and couldn't see any sign of Borovsky. However, he had no idea what kind of car he was driving. I'm sure he's here somewhere, because he left Zurich before I did. Perhaps he's up on the mountain. I hope so, he thought. If I hurry, I can get these ladies out of here before he shows up. Finally, they'll be safe. Son of a gun, after all this chasing around, I certainly didn't think this would end so easily. He had a slight smile on his face.

When the two women approached their car, Tony stepped out in front of them. "Are you Katherine Wilson and Pauline Maddich?"

They straightened up in surprise and took a step back. Katherine shoulders slumped "Not again," she mumbled.

"I can't take much more of this," Pauline wailed.

"Ladies, ladies, you're safe. I'm Tony Cappelli. I'm with the CIA. I'm here to get you to safety."

Katherine squinted her eyes as she looked at Tony's black hair and swarthy complexion. "Cappelli? That's

Italian, isn't it?" She turned to Pauline. "Oh, brother. Now we have the Mafia chasing us."

Tony rolled his eyes. The FBI was right. These two are *fruitcakes*. "Katherine, you've been watching too many reruns of *The Godfather*. I really am from the CIA. We know you've been mistaken for Russian arms dealers and were given diamonds by mistake. We've been trying to make contact with you ever since Paris. Here let me show you my badge and identification." He opened the right side of his suit coat and was reaching into the inside pocket to retrieve his identification.

Everything seemed to happen simultaneously. When Tony opened his suit coat, Katherine spotted his gun in the shoulder holster. She shouted, "Gun!" And at the very same instant, she brought her right leg back and then forward using all the strength she had.

Shouting, "Yee Ah!" just like her self-defense instructor taught her, she whipped her leg forward with all her might and her foot hit Tony right in the nuts.

Without a sound, Tony dropped to the ground. But as he was plummeting, in that nanosecond before the excruciating pain enveloped his entire being, he had one thought . . . *I'm going to kill her.*

Without waiting, Katherine bent down and pulled Tony's gun out of the holster. He made a feeble attempt to stop her, but didn't have the strength.

Pauline was frozen to the spot. It took a few seconds for her to process all that had happened within the short time span. She stood there looking down at the poor man who was now moaning. As a nurse, she knew there was nothing she could do for him. He just had to wait it out. *This is surreal This can't be happening.*

She turned to Katherine with a wild look on her face. "Why did you do that?" she shouted.

"I had to do it, Pauline. He had a gun." She held it up to show her and then stuffed it in her purse. She snatched the car keys out of Pauline's hand.

"I'm driving. Get in the car. We've got to get out of here." She jerked open the driver's door and jumped in. "Would you get in the car," she hissed at Pauline before she slammed her door shut and started the engine.

Pauline pulled herself out of the paralysis and ran to the passenger's side. Before she had her door closed, Katherine had the car in reverse and was backing up. She threw it into drive. With wheels spinning, she sped out of the parking lot.

CHAPTER 26

The ascending car had now arrived at the boarding platform and the people in line started to move forward to board. Dimitri checked to see where the women were. When he looked out on the parking lot, he spotted Tony Cappelli standing next to the women's car. He stopped trying to work his way down the ramp. He didn't know if Tony knew who he was, so he didn't want to approach them and confuse the issue by interfering with getting those women to safety. He looked up at the car taking on passengers that would be descending. If Ivan was on it because he figured out the ladies were no longer on the mountain, he did not want to be exposed standing here on the lower boarding ramp. However, because the descending car would not begin its travel down until the ascending car began to travel up, he felt he had time before exiting the ramp. Standing along side the railing, he waited to see what would happen.

He watched Tony speak to them and then he saw what Katherine did to Tony. A look of commensurate pain crossed Dimitri's face as Tony dropped to the ground. "Oooooo," he said softly. Unconsciously, his hands moved down to cover his privates. After a moment, he realized what he had done. He gave his head a small shake and brought his hands back to the railing. When the women jumped into their car and proceeded to race out of the parking lot, he had to make a quick decision. Should he go to his car and follow them or should he go over and help Tony? He went to help Tony. If Ivan was on the descending car, he didn't want him to catch sight of Tony lying there.

Tony was still on the ground, when he arrived. He knelt beside him. "I am Dimitri Zarenko. I saw what just happened. I assume the ladies took your gun also." He was smiling as he looked down at Tony.

"Oh, shit." Tony muttered slowly fighting to get each word out. He was still in agonizing pain.

Demitri had a twinkle in his eyes. "I know this is embarrassing. But the more I chase those two ladies the more I am fascinated by them. Listen, Borovsky is at the top of the mountain. He could be coming down any time now. Can you move? We need to get you on the side of your car, so he doesn't see us when he gets here."

Tony rolled over on his side and pushed himself into a sitting position. He took in gulps of air and blew them out through his mouth. The intense pain was finally receding somewhat. Dimitri grabbed him under the arms and helped slide him to the side of the car. He leaned Tony against the back door then he raised his head above the hood and scanned the lot. The cable car was slowly approaching the departure platform.

"Stay down. A cable car is about to reach the platform. Ivan may be on it." After a few minutes, he saw Ivan and Helmut get out of the car. "The idiot!" he hissed. "Ivan has his gun out in plain sight." Dimitri pulled out his gun and had it at his side as he waited. He looked over at the frantic look on Tony's face. "Do not worry. There will be no American cowboy shoot-outs. Unless Ivan sees us, I do not intend to use this." He nodded toward the gun at his side.

Meanwhile, Tony turned and got on his knees. He raised his head and looked through the car window. He saw Borovsky running to his car waving his gun in the direction of the empty slot where the women's car had been. He and Dimitri ducked down. Borovsky and Helmut got in their car and drove out of the lot. When they were out of sight, Tony used the car to help him stand. The worst was over.

"You need to go after them, Dimitri. Borovsky can't get to those women." Now that Tony was able to form thoughts again, his mind began racing. He took out his cell phone. "Give me your phone number so we can stay in touch." He punched in the numbers as Dimitri called them off.

"When I ended up in the hospital in Amsterdam, Ivan did not believe me. And because I did not catch the women, he accused me of being a traitor and fired me." Dimitri looked over at Tony and shook his head in disgust. "I will to try to contact him again while I am driving. Getting back with Ivan may be difficult, but I will see what I can do," Dimitri said. "I need to be able to tell him something that will make him trust me again."

He pulled out his car keys and proceeded to talk to Tony as he was backing up across the lot to his car. "Maybe I can talk some sense into him. But if I cannot, at least I can follow him and keep him from hurting those ladies. Henri told me the two women are trying to reach Vienna and the American Embassy. I will tell Ivan I am already in Vienna and want to meet him there.

You and I will keep in touch and figure out what to do as we drive." He turned and hurried to his car.

Moments later, Tony cautiously got in his car and drove out behind Dimitri. Once on the road, he punched in the number for Henri to let him know what had happened. Hopefully, Henri could begin to monitor the women's car once they got onto a major highway. If the electronic monitors break down on the way to Vienna like they did in Zurich, I'm going to scream, he thought while waiting for Henri to answer.

CHAPTER 27

Katherine and Pauline had not said one word to each other as they sped down the road. Several miles after they left the cable car parking lot, Katherine took an off ramp and drove down a country road.

None of the pursuers were aware of the ladies' detour. They were too far behind them. Borovsky's car shot past the ramp and continued on. Dimitri sped past the ramp following Ivan. And, Tony drove past while he was on the phone to Henri.

Katherine pulled the car to the side of the road and shut off the engine. She held on to the steering wheel with both hands and stared straight ahead. Her teeth began to chatter.

Pauline looked over at her friend and realized something was very wrong. She tried humor. "You can always try shouting *ka-ka-poo-poo.*" When Katherine did not respond, but kept staring out the window taking short shallow breaths, she became very alarmed. If she couldn't reach her with a joke, this was bad.

She grabbed Katherine's arm and gave it a slight shake. "Katherine!" she said in a loud voice. "Don't you dare give up now. You're the one who has gotten us through all this. You're the one who has been strong for both of us. I need you. Come on, Katherine."

Katherine laid her head on the steering wheel. "Oh, Pauline. I'm sorry. It just got to be too much. Now we're being chased by the Mafia for crying out loud. With guns, again!" Tears rolled down her cheeks. She wiped them away with her sleeve. She leaned back against the seat and turned her head toward Pauline and gave her a weak smile. "Sorry, kiddo. But I just needed to do that. Honest to goodness, Pauline, what the hell is going on? Things like this only happen in the movies not in real life." She was so exasperated. "This isn't who we are. We don't live like this."

Pauline put her arms around her and held her. "I know, I know," she said softly. "We'll sit here for a minute and just regroup."

Katherine inhaled and blew the air out slowly. She was getting herself back under control again. "This has to end. We have to get to Vienna by the end of today."

She took her cell phone out of her purse and turned it on. She was going to look up the mileage to Vienna to determine how long it would take them to get there. Once her phone connected, it started ringing. She looked at her email file and saw she had an email from her daughter, Priscilla. "Oh, no. It's from Priscilla. I'm almost afraid to open it." She clicked on it.

EMAIL
From: Priscilla Wilson
To: Katherine Wilson

Mom – enough is enough. We have to know you're okay. Answer your phone and quit fooling around. Do you know how scary it is to have the FBI at your house telling you your mother is involved in a Russian arms deal!!!!!!!!!!!!!! And, hearing your mother talk about having a GUN!!!!!!!!!!!!!!

You pick up that phone and CALL me. We need to know you're OK. Independence is one thing, but terrifying your children is not right. Please Mom . . .

I do love you,
Priscilla

"Aw, we're really scaring the kids. I have to answer her and let her know we're okay." She began writing a reply.

EMAIL
To: Priscilla Wilson
From: Katherine Wilson

Please don't worry about us, Honey. I promise you, Pauline and I are safe. We're taking care of the situation. Right now we are on our way to Vienna. We are going to go to the American Embassy to get help. So please don't worry. Everything will be fine. I'll tell you all about this when I get back. But, again, please don't worry.

Love, Mom

When she pressed send, her phone rang again. She looked at the caller ID of the incoming call. She sat up straight, held the phone to her chest and glanced at Pauline. "Oh, no. It's Arthur," she said in a whisper.

"Well, answer it." Pauline had a slight smile on her face.

"What am I going to say to him?" The phone kept ringing. Her face was screwed up in a scared, questioning look.

"Oh, come on, *Diamond Lil*. Think of something. And, put it on speaker phone, I want to hear this." Pauline's eyes twinkled and there was a silly grin on her face.

Katherine hit answer and put the call on speaker. "Hello," she said in a timid voice.

"Katherine! My god, what's happening over there? I got a phone call from Priscilla saying you're involved in an arms deal? And something about having a gun? I have been trying to reach you for days but only got your voice mail. I thought something happened to you. Are you all right?"

"Yes, yes, we're okay, Arthur. I have to admit we have had quite an adventure. But, we've got it under control now. We're on our way to the American Embassy in Vienna to, ah, turn ourselves in."

"Do you need me, Katherine? Do you want me to fly over there? I'll do whatever you need me to do."

Because Pauline had told Katherine that Arthur looked at her as if she was lunch, she began to mimic eating a sandwich. Her eyes twinkled with mirth. Katherine gave her a snarling look and mouthed, "Stop it".

"No, you stay put. This should all be over by tomorrow."

"This whole thing sounds like more than your usual caper, Katherine. And when I couldn't reach you, I became so worried. Now, what is going on, My Dear? Please tell me."

It was like the flood gates had opened when Arthur said that. "Oh, Arthur. We don't really know what's going on. We were having such a grand time in England. But then within hours of reaching Paris everything got weird. Some man gave us a million dollars in diamonds! A million dollars, for heaven's sake. And, we don't know why he did that. Do you know how hard it is to carry a million dollars in diamonds around in your bra? That was Pauline's idea. She thought it was the safest place. It's been almost two weeks. I'm telling you, Arthur, our boobs have so many pock marks from those diamonds shoved down there, they look like four dying sponges on a coral reef."

The women could hear Arthur begin to laugh uproariously.

"Now men with guns are chasing us and trying to get the diamonds back. This morning we found out we now have the Mafia chasing us, and we picked up another gun! We're on our way to Vienna to get to the American Embassy. Hopefully, they'll be able to help us and make all the bad guys stop chasing us." She seemed to run out of steam and stopped talking.

The laughing stopped. Arthur became serious. "Where are you now?" he asked.

"Somewhere in Lichtenstein. I was just going to check to see how many more miles we have to go to reach Vienna when I received your phone call."

"All right, Katherine, while you two are on your way to Vienna, I'm going to pull some strings over here and see if I can find out just what's happening to you and why that man gave you the diamonds. And, I'm going to see if I can find out exactly who is chasing you. I have some old college friends I still keep in contact with who used to work at the State Department in Washington. They should be able to help."

"Thank you, Arthur. You're a good friend."

Pauline rolled her eyes and gave Katherine a disgusted look. "You're a good friend," she mouthed mockingly. Katherine gave her another snarling look.

"Well, I hope you consider me more than just a good friend, Katherine."

"Yes," Pauline whispered with a smile on her face as she closed her eyes, made a fist and brought her arm down.

"Now, I want you to keep your phone on so I can reach you once I have more information. Will you do that for me?"

"Yes."

"And, I want you to call me when you are safe at the Embassy. I don't think I'll sleep well until I know you're okay."

"All right. I promise to let you know."

"Good-bye, My Dear," Arthur said.

"Good-bye, My, ah . . . My, it was good to hear your voice," she added weakly. She couldn't add the "my dear" part quite yet.

She ended the call and sat there for a moment looking out the front window. "Well, that was awkward."

"I told you he was crazy about you," Pauline squealed like a high school teenager at a pep rally.

Katherine just rolled her eyes. But she did have a slight smile on her face. After a moment she straightened and gave her head a shake. "All right. I'm back under control." She reached down and brought her purse up to her lap. She took out Tony's gun and examined it. It looked like the safety was on. She lowered Pauline's window that faced the open field and handed her the gun. "Here. See this little lever on the side? I'm quite sure it's the safety," she said pointing at the gun.

"But, we've got to make sure, so I'm going to push this lever. Now I want you to fire the gun out the window to see what happens."

Pauline recoiled. "No way am I going to fire that gun! Why do you keep taking everyone's gun?"

She continued to hold the gun out to her friend. "Fire the damn gun, Pauline!" Katherine shouted with such force that Pauline reached over and timidly took the gun.

"Oh, yuck. This is the worst day of my life. She held the gun out the window, turned her face away, scrunched her eyes shut and squeezed the trigger.

Kaboom! The gun went off. Pauline's hand flew up from the recoil and the gun fell to the ground outside of the car.

"Oh, my God! Not again," Pauline shouted at Katherine.

"Go get the gun," Katherine said. "Because now I am going to push the lever the other way, and I want you to fire again."

"No way," Pauline said. She folded her arms and glared at Katherine.

"We can't leave the loaded gun lying there, Pauline. Someone may find it and use it. Now go get the gun and we'll try it again only this time we'll push the lever back to where it was."

Pauline got out of the car and picked the gun up by the handle with two fingers. "I hate you for making me do this," Pauline said. "Why don't you get out here and fire it?" Katherine just sat there and waited.

Pauline gave Katherine a murderous look and got back in the car. Resigned to the fact that she was going to have to fire it again, she held it out the window while she pushed the lever back to its original position.

Again she turned her face away, scrunched her eyes shut and squeezed the trigger. This time nothing happened. She opened her eyes and looked at the gun.

Then she turned away, shut her eyes, and tried again. The trigger wouldn't budge. "Thank God, the lever is the safety," she said and handed the gun back to Katherine.

"No. I can't carry both. They're too heavy. You keep that one in your purse." She gave Pauline a "don't you dare refuse" look.

"Oooh. This is just awful," she said. She carefully placed the gun in her purse making sure nothing would snag on the safety lever. She gently set the purse on the floor.

Katherine retrieved her cell phone and began typing. "We need to know how many miles we have to drive to get to Vienna. The map shows 323 miles. Okay, I figure ball-park, one hour for every fifty miles. So it should take us about seven hours to get there." Checking the time on her phone, she mentally counted off the hours. "It's a little before noon now, so we should be in Vienna early this evening." She started the car, made a u-turn and headed back to the highway going north.

CHAPTER 28

Tony made good time on the route out of the mountains. He was getting close to the German border. His cell phone rang. Caller ID indicated it was Henri.

"Yeah, Henri. What's going on? Were you able to track everyone? Where are the women?" he asked.

"As you Americans say, I have some good news and I have some bad news. Which do you want first?"

"Oh brother. Give me the bad news first."

"We can't locate the women anywhere."

"What?" The word seemed to explode out of his mouth. "What do you mean you can't locate them?"

"We have not been able to pick up their car anywhere on the highway. Right now, we are tracking your car and Zarenko's and Borovsky's," Henri said.

"Jeez, Henri, this whole thing is turning into a three-ringed circus, for crying-out-loud. Thousands of satellites floating around in space that can watch a man take a piss in Outer Mongolia, yet we can't find two little old ladies within a fifty-mile radius here. What the hell." By now Tony was yelling, he was so frustrated.

"Take it easy, Tony. We are trying one more thing. We have decided to try scanning the area to see if we can pick up any activity on the women's cell phones. Remember they have had their phone off for days? Since we were not getting any signals for two days after they shut them off, we stopped monitoring. We felt it was useless to continue. But now we are trying again. Wait a minute, Tony, someone is trying to talk to me." Henri put his hand over the mouthpiece.

Tony could hear muffled voices while he waited impatiently. This was the most frustrating assignment I have ever been on, he thought. How can those two ditzy, old ladies keep eluding all of us? He shook his head in bewilderment. He started to review all the times they just slipped away. After a moment, he thought, maybe that's it. If they were professionals, they would be making all the anticipated clandestine moves, and we would've been able to nab them by now. But, these two loonies are just acting *normal* and it's confusing the hell out of us. He started to smile then he began to laugh quietly as he waited for Henri to come back on the phone.

"Tony? Are you still there?"

"Yeah, I'm here, Henri."

"We just picked up cell phone activity on Katherine's phone. We are zeroing in on their location and trying to get in to monitor their calls."

"Well, where the hell are they?" Tony asked.

"You are not going to like this. They are about thirty-five kilometers *behind* you."

"Behind me? Are you kidding?" Tony roared. "How did they get behind me? They were the first ones out of the parking lot. The three of us pulled out *after* they left and followed them."

"Well, from what we can see by the cell phone location, they are no longer on the highway. They must have pulled off shortly after they left the parking lot and are now on a side road. No, wait hold it. There they are. I am looking at the highway monitor right now. They just drove back onto the highway and are going north, thank goodness. They are keeping to the route the young woman in Zurich told us they would be taking, so that is one good thing. Let me check to see exactly where you are. All right, if you get off on the next exit and let them go by, you can get back on and be behind them. I will tell you when they pass your exit. We will keep an eye on Zarenko and Borovsky to make sure they do not get close to you or the ladies."

"All right. I see it. I'll be coming up to the off ramp shortly," Tony told Henri when he spotted the sign. "I'll take it and wait. Let me know when they go past then I'll follow them all the way to Vienna. It'll be easier to confront them there than here in the middle of nowhere. The way these ladies keep slipping away, we'll probably have to call out the entire Austrian Army for help."

Henri laughed. "If it wasn't for the seriousness of Borovsky in the picture, this would be quite enjoyable." They were quiet as they waited for the ladies to catch up with Tony.

"Okay, just a few more minutes and they will pass your ramp. Are you ready?"

"Yeah, I'm waiting on the side of the on-ramp now."

When the women drove past, Tony got in behind them and began to tail them. Henri was in the process of checking the cell phone activity and told Tony he would call back as soon as possible.

Now that things were somewhat under control, Tony had a chance to do some serious thinking as he drove. The important thing we have to consider is – if we pick up Borovsky before he gets near the women that'll stop him from harming them, but that way he walks. We have nothing to charge him with. Nada, zip, nothing. And, he has got to be stopped. Dimitri is right. Ivan is no longer sane. He can't be allowed to continue.

He wiped his hand over his face as he continued with his thoughts. So that means we have to let him get to the women and then arrest him. Once we arrest him for kidnapping, it'll mean warrants will be issued allowing us to look deeper into his business activities. Then we bring him down for good.

But can we protect the women when he grabs them? Running around the cable car parking lot with his gun in plain sight proves he really is dangerous. Will he shoot them as soon as he sees them, even if it's out in the open and on the street? They don't deserve to die or even be harmed for that matter. They're just innocent bystanders in this whole mess.

He called Henri. He needed to discuss his concerns with him to see if it was feasible to get Borovsky and at the same time keep the women safe. After Henri listened to Tony's ideas, he patched in Dimitri for a three-way call so they could discuss this issue.

Dimitri told them he was in contact with Ivan again and they planned to meet up in Vienna. He suggested he wear some sort of tracking device before he reached

Ivan. That way, Tony and Henri would be able to know where Ivan was at all times. Tony said he could get him a watch to wear that had a GPS devise in it. He suggested Dimitri meet him at the American Embassy. Dimitri gave a slight chuckle. He said with his reputation, entering the Embassy would not be a good idea. They chose a coffee shop located two blocks from the Embassy.

Dimitri also added if Ivan did take the women, he would probably take them to a warehouse he owned on the outskirts of Vienna. He gave them the address.

Henri decided he would fly to Vienna. He could be there by late afternoon, since the flight would only take a little over an hour. He felt if he were there, he could better work with the Viennese police and his counterpart at Interpol. They could reconnoiter the warehouse and get men in place just in case Ivan brought the women there.

"What if these women drive into Vienna and go straight to the Embassy?" Tony asked. "We're making plans as if they are going to wait and go to the Embassy tomorrow giving Borovsky a chance to grab them."

There was silence on the three phones. Then Henri spoke softly. "Well, then it is over. Is it not? We will not be able to get Borovsky, but the women will be safe. *C'est la Vie.*"

Tony shook his head. "No. We need to assume the women will check into a hotel tonight and go to the Embassy tomorrow. Better to have plans in place for the worse case scenario. I don't want to be scrambling around tomorrow morning and risk the lives of those women. Now I have to get off this phone call and contact my counterpart in Vienna and let her know what needs to be done as soon as possible."

"Can I add one thing before you hang up?" Dimitri asked. "Once I meet with Ivan, that will be it for me. I will have to stay with him. He will get suspicious if I try to leave. So I will need the watch before I go to him and I will need to know whatever basic plans you have made."

"All right, Dimitri. I can arrange that." Tony wished he were at his desk so he could be taking notes. "After I contact our Embassy, I'll call you and let you know when and where you can get the watch and what we have decided to do."

"I will do the same, Dimitri," Henri added. "And, I will continue to monitor the women's cell phone. We should be able to trace any calls they make."

Once the phone call ended, both Tony and Henri were back on their phones calling their counterparts in Vienna to alert them to what was about to happen.

CHAPTER 29

At seven o'clock that evening, Tony was smiling as he sat in his car watching Katherine and Pauline walk through the door of the hotel in Vienna to check in. Now just sit tight, ladies, so we can complete our plans to keep you safe.

Henri had called him this afternoon and told him they traced a call from Pauline's cell phone to the hotel in Vienna. The Interpol police in Vienna confirmed they had made a reservation for this evening at the hotel located three blocks away from the American Embassy. Once Henri arrived in Vienna at 4:30 p.m. that afternoon, he arranged a police stakeout at the hotel.

"Good," Tony told Henri. "The women should be safe for the rest of the evening. Even if they do leave the hotel for some reason, they'll have police following them."

He started the car and pulled out into traffic. Now it was time for him to check in at the Embassy. Thank goodness, I know my CIA counterpart here in Vienna. It will be good to see Edie again, he thought. They had shared their first assignment together at the Embassy in Oslo.

He pulled into the Embassy parking area. Thoughts about Norway came flooding back. Walking up to the front steps, he thought about how cocky they were in Norway even though they were only raw recruits. He chuckled thinking about the time they were chewed out by their boss for coming to work with raging hangovers. The night before, they drank Aquavit for the first time and nearly ended up under the table on their kiesters.

The only problem with Edie will be explaining why I need to requisition a new gun. He winced at the thought. I'm hoping she let herself go and is fat now. It'll be easier to tell her about the gun if she really is fat and out of shape. My luck, she probably works out and could pose for a spread in *Cosmopolitan*. Won't I look like a complete wimp telling her why my gun was taken from me, and worse yet, how it was taken by two 71 year-old women. Geez.

When he got to the secured entrance of the Embassy, the Marine Guard behind the bulletproof glass pushed open the metal drawer. Tony emptied his pockets and laid his CIA identification on top. The guard pulled the drawer closed and reached for the identification. After he examined it and realized Tony was CIA, he slide the drawer back open again and told Tony he had to put his gun in the drawer. Tony told him he wasn't carrying a gun.

That's when the Marine put his hand on his side arm and gave Tony a hard stare. Somehow he must have pushed a button under the counter, because two Marines came out of a side door on the other side of the electronic walk-through in front of Tony. Security was very, very tight at all Embassies around the world. He knew it was very suspicious when a man claiming to be a CIA agent was not carrying a gun. Tony couldn't blame them for their reaction to him.

"Would you please call Edie Patterson? She will identify who I am," Tony told the guard.

After a few minutes Edie entered the area on the other side of the electronic walk-through and told the Marines, she knew him and Tony could enter.

"Why don't you have your gun?" she asked as Tony passed through the electronic arch. "Too much Aquavit last night?" Tony smiled. Edie must be having the same memories.

"Let's go to your office. I'll tell you all about it there," Tony answered.

They took the stairs to the second floor. Edie's office was the third one on the left. Before they went in, they stopped in the kitchen area and each got a cup of coffee. Even though it was already eight o'clock at night, coffee seemed to be a necessary part of any clandestine work.

There was a meeting area in the corner of Edie's office with two stuffed chairs and a small round table between them. Each took a chair and put their coffee mugs on the table.

Edie gave Tony questioning look. "Now, you want to tell me what's going on?" she asked. "And, who the hell are these two women? Because I've got to tell you, two hours ago, I got a phone call from the State Department in Washington for God's sake. They want to know what's happening with the women." She reached into the side pocket of her suit, pulled out a piece of paper and handed it to Tony.

"Here's the number and contact person in Washington. You need to call him and bring him up to speed."

Tony blew out a very large breath of air as if he had been kicked in the stomach. He couldn't believe this whole thing would go so high up the chain. Good grief, he thought. Edie's right. 'Who the hell are these women?'

"I don't know what to say, Edie. I thought we were working with just average American citizens." He looked down at the piece of paper. "The State Department," he whispered. It was a question and a statement. When he looked up, he had a bewildered look on his face.

"Well, come on. Let's get you to a secure phone, so you can make the phone call. I'll go with you. That way you won't have to waste time repeating the story. And," Edie gave him a wink. "You can fill me in later on all the things you didn't include to the State Department." Tony raised his eyebrows and gave her a smirk.

CHAPTER 30

Katherine and Pauline were exhausted after the long and harrowing drive from Lichtenstein. Other than getting gas, they hadn't stopped once even for food. But just being in Vienna finally felt safe to them. They decided to check into a hotel, take a breather, and go to the Embassy in the morning. They had eaten dinner in the hotel restaurant and were now back in their room relaxing on their beds watching the BBC news on T.V. The BBC reporter was giving an update of yet another bombing in a far-off war ravaged country.

"You know one of the things I like about traveling is we don't have access to the news quite so much. It's nice to be able spend a few days thinking all is right with the world without having to be bombarded with another bombing, another shooting, or more hatred," Pauline said.

"I've thought the same thing," Katherine replied. "I think a lot of the uneasiness we feel in the world today can be blamed directly on the news media. Think about it. With modern technology we now have access to world events almost instantaneously. And by media standards, the more horrible the event, the more air time it gets. It's precisely those things coming into our homes on a daily basis twenty-four seven that makes it seem as if the violence and the hatred happening thousands of miles away is really right outside our door. It doesn't make any difference what country you live in. The news media is reporting the same types of news. All people are uneasy."

"That's an interesting take on what's happening," Pauline said.

Just then Katherine's cell phone rang. It was Arthur.

"Arthur," Katherine said when she answered it.

Arthur wasted no time. He began peppering her with questions. "Where are you? Are you safe now? Were the two of you able to reach the Embassy?"

"Wait a minute, Arthur. I'm going to put you on speaker so Pauline can hear you too." She pushed speaker and put the phone down on the nightstand.

"First, we're safe. We haven't made it to the Embassy yet. We decided to calm down and spend the night in a hotel. It's located a few blocks away from the Embassy."

"Well, my dear, you two have gotten yourselves into quite a kerfuffle to say the least. I just got off the phone . . . Wait, I'm sorry. I forgot my manners. Pauline? How are you?" Arthur asked.

"I'm fine, Arthur. Now please tell us what this is all about. We can't take much more of this."

"As I was saying, I just got off the phone with a former classmate of mine who worked at the State Department. He said you two were mistaken for the mother and aunt of a very nasty and notorious Russian arms dealer whose name is Ivan Borovsky. Apparently, his gun buyer tailed you all the way from London thinking you were the Russian's mother and aunt."

"Why on earth would the man think that?" Pauline asked.

"Well, because the real mother and aunt missed the Eurostar. The same one you two were on. Somehow the two of you sat in the other ladies seats on the train. When the buyer saw who was sitting in the correct seats, he assumed you were Borovsky's mother and aunt. Think about it. Not only were you in their seats, you two also fit the profile of being the right age."

"Oh, good grief. Remember when we decided to switch to the window seats? Those must have been their seats. And it was so innocent too." Katherine looked over at Pauline and rolled her eyes.

"Then to make matters worse, you checked into the George Cinq in Paris. The gun buyer knew the mother and aunt always stayed at the Cinq."

Pauline squinted her eyes at Katherine. "You made us stay there."

"Not only that," he continued. "You went to the exact café where the other women were supposed to go to collect the diamonds."

Katherine gave Pauline a haughty look. "Ha. You're the one who chose that café." Pauline gave her a disgusted look.

"Once the two of you got the diamonds, the chase was on. Right now, you are being followed by Borovsky, Interpol and the CIA. All of them want the diamonds back. By the way, Katherine, at the cable car in Lichtenstein, I believe the man you kicked in the, ah, shall we say, family jewels, actually was from the CIA."

"But he was Italian! And, he had a gun," Katherine quickly responded trying to vindicate herself.

Pauline just curled her lip in a snarl. "We could have been safe by now," she muttered.

"Well, what about the man who pointed the gun at us in Amsterdam?" Katherine asked.

"Amsterdam?" Arthur asked. "I didn't get any information about a man in Amsterdam. Do you want me to call my friend back and find out more about him?"

No, never mind, Arthur," Pauline said. "You've helped us understand the situation now. Thank you."

"Now ladies, it's your turn. Exactly when are you planning to go to the Embassy?" Arthur asked.

"We didn't get into Vienna until almost seven this evening and we're exhausted. We need time to get ourselves under control again," Katherine said,

"And this late at night, we thought the Embassy would be closed," Pauline added. "So we're going to go there first thing in the morning."

Arthur gave a slight cough. "It's too late now to say this, but I assure you the Embassy is never closed. The door may be locked, but there is always a guard at the entrance. Please promise me the two of you will get to the Embassy tomorrow morning as soon as possible." The two nodded emphatically at each other.

"Don't delay. As I understand it, this Russian man is a very nasty person. You don't want to give him a chance to get near you." Katherine and Pauline looked across the table at each other. Neither was happy to learn how dangerous this mess really was.

"All right, Arthur. Thanks for helping us understand what this is all about. We'll call you tomorrow when we're safe," Katherine said.

Good night, to both of you," Arthur said and hung up the phone.

Pauline rubbed her forehead with her fingers. "Well, this is worse than we thought, isn't it?"

"At least we know what's going on now," Katherine added. "But, yikes, this is scary."

"What do we do with the guns when we go to the Embassy?" Pauline raised her eyes and looked at her friend. "Can't leave them here in the hotel."

Katherine shrugged her shoulders. "I say we take them with us. We'll just march up to the front door of the Embassy and do what Avon does. We ring the doorbell. When they answer, we tell them we have guns. Then let the Embassy figure out what to do with them."

She paused and looked around the room for a few moments. "We need to lock ourselves in the room for the night." Checking the door, she said, "The door has a dead-bolt. But, to be sure, let's wedge a chair under the handle." She gave a quiet snort. "Then we try to get some sleep."

Pauline rubbed her forehead again. "Praying might be a good idea too."

CHAPTER 31

Tony wasn't getting much sleep in his room at the Embassy. He kept tossing and turning all night. At 5:00 a.m. he finally gave up and got out of bed. As he was taking a shower and getting dressed, he ran the plans allowing Borovsky to kidnap the women through his head over and over. And every single time, he came to the same conclusion. He couldn't let Borovsky get to the women. It had nothing to do with the fact the issue had gone up to the State Department. It had to do with the fact that if Borovsky killed those ladies, their deaths would haunt him for the rest of his life. It simply wasn't worth it. Sooner or later Ivan would be caught, but not today. He grabbed his cell phone and went down to the cafeteria for breakfast.

He wasn't all that hungry so he just got a cup of coffee. After he had taken a few sips, he called Henri. I hope he's awake, he thought while dialing. Unfortunately, Henri was still asleep when he called, but became alert quickly as Tony was speaking.

"Henri, I can't do it. I can't let Borovsky get to those women. Catching him isn't worth risking their lives. I had a phone call from our State Department last night. The man told me the women plan to come to the Embassy this morning for help. So I'm driving over to the hotel around seven. I'll park in the street on the north side. Somewhere where I can keep an eye on the hotel entrance. I want to be in my car in case, God forbid, something goes wrong and I need to move fast. With those two slippery characters, I'm leaving nothing to chance. And I don't want to be standing on the sidewalk either. If they spot me, they'll probably get spooked and run in the opposite direction of the Embassy. I want this over."

"I agree with you. I will be there at seven also. And I will park somewhere near you to wait. Don't forget there are two men from Interpol in the hotel lobby. If the women leave the hotel for any reason, the men are instructed to follow them. With you and I and the men from Interpol, the women should be well protected. See you in a few hours."

After Tony hung up, he dialed Edie's phone to tell her of his decision not to put the women in jeopardy. He woke her up too.

She sat up in bed as he was speaking. "I'll go with you, Tony. I'll meet you in the entrance at six forty-five. Actually, I wouldn't miss this for the world. Lord knows someone has to be there to protect you in case those two senior citizen thugs attack you again and take your gun."

He winced when she said that. Yesterday he thought Edie would never stop laughing when he told her how the women got his gun.

"Not funny. And, if you ever tell anyone about this, I will never forgive you." He could actually hear her begin to snicker. Irritated, he ended the call without saying good-bye.

For a few minutes he sat quietly staring across the room. I've made the right decision, he thought. In less than two hours this will all be over. The women will finally be safe. We'll have the diamonds. Borovsky will still be running around, but we'll just keep a better eye on him and shut him down once and for all later. Having made this decision, he realized he was famished now. He rose, went to the breakfast bar and filled his plate.

The two women were getting dressed for their big day. Katherine was in the process of shoving the diamonds down in her bra. "I'm sick of being so uncomfortable. I don't think these pucker marks are ever going to come out. Thank goodness, this craziness is finally going to be over."

"Is this outfit okay or should I change?" Pauline asked while checking herself out in the mirror. "What does one wear to the Embassy? Maybe I should be a little more dressy."

"Oh, for crying out loud, Pauline. It doesn't really matter what you wear. This isn't a diplomatic ball we're going to. We're going there to drop off two guns and a million dollars in diamonds. For that, you look fine."

"Well, I just want to be sure." Pauline said. She pulled on the sleeves of her jacket and straightened the collar of her blouse. Then she ran a brush through her hair.

When they were in the elevator, Pauline turned and said, "We're going to have breakfast before we go."

"Why?" Katherine asked dumbfounded. "Listen, we need to get to that Embassy. No fooling around here. We can eat later." Pauline was acting funny. What's going on, she thought.

"Who knows when we'll get a chance to eat? So I want to do it now."

"Good grief, kiddo. We're going to the Embassy not to prison, you know. There'll be time to eat later."

"No," Pauline said with finality.

The elevator reached the lobby. They got out. When they passed the hotel gift shop on their way to the restaurant, Pauline made a u-turn and headed back to the shop. "Just a minute. I have to get something." She entered and walked over to the display of Swarovski crystal.

"What the heck are you doing now?" Katherine was losing her patience. Her friend's behavior was really beginning to upset her.

"I need to buy this crystal clown." Pauline said pointing to a little two-inch clown that sparkled on the glass shelf.

"What?" Katherine asked in exasperation. It was just a teeny, tiny clown, for heavens sakes. She didn't know what to make of her friend's odd behavior. "Why are you buying that dumb clown at a time like this?"

Pauline stood in front of the display case holding the clown. She looked down at it and then turned to her friend. "I don't know why I'm doing this. It just seems like something I have to do."

At the counter and she took out her credit card to pay for the crystal.

Katherine frowned again. "Why are you using your credit card? Just charge it to our room? We need to be on our way."

"No," Pauline answered. "This way when we pay the hotel bill, we'll each pay half and won't have to worry about divvying up my charge."

Katherine screwed up her face and slowly shook her head in total confusion as she watched her friend.

The sales clerk slid the charge card through and completed the transaction.

Ping... Within minutes, several miles away Borovsky now knew where the women were. As soon as Helmut zeroed in on Pauline's credit card transaction, Ivan grabbed him and Dimitri and was out the door to get the women.

Because Pauline did not give up on the fact she wanted to eat breakfast before they set out for the Embassy, they were now seated at the table in the hotel restaurant. When their breakfast was served, each of them picked at their food. They realized they weren't really hungry.

Katherine reached across the table and took Pauline's hand. "Are you okay?" she asked looking at her friend with a great deal of concern.

Pauline's shoulders slumped. "Yeah, I'm okay." She squeezed Katherine's hand and gave her friend a sheepish smile. "I don't know what came over me this morning. Well, yes I do. Katherine, I'm scared. I just want everyone to stop chasing us. I want to stop collecting guns wherever we go. And I want to stop making all these getaways from every city we visit." She picked up the bag from the gift shop and shook her head. She gave an embarrassing laugh. "And, I still have no idea why I needed this stupid clown."

Katherine patted her hand. "You had me worried there for a minute. All right, take a deep breath. And since we've paid for this food, let's try to eat something. Then we're out of here." She checked her watch. "Think about it. In thirty minutes, this will all be over. We'll be safe in the Embassy."

CHAPTER 32

Tony met Edie in the front entry of the Embassy at quarter to seven. They took his car. When they left, Tony drove just two blocks down the street and parked. He was one block away from the hotel when he pulled to the curb. From here he could see the hotel entrance, and he felt he was well situated between the hotel and the Embassy. A few minutes later, Henri pulled in behind him. They gave each other a wave of acknowledgement through their windows.

"You know, Edie, I'm not going to feel comfortable until these two nut-jobs are actually inside the Embassy. I think I have all the bases covered, but the way things have been going for the past several weeks, everything could change in a New York minute."

Edie was watching the hotel entrance. "Before we left, I spoke to the duty officer who's monitoring Zarenko on the GPS. He said Zarenko was still sitting tight a few miles from here. So you don't have to worry about Borovsky."

But then two things happened. Katherine and Pauline had finished their breakfast and were walking through the lobby on their way out of the hotel. They were fortunate enough to slip in front of a large group of German tourists who had just checked out and were also exiting. But the policemen from Interpol, who were assigned to protect the women, weren't so lucky. They spotted the women coming out of the restaurant and by the time they reacted, they ended up having to exit the hotel *behind* the German group.

While this was going on, Edie's cell phone rang. "Hello. You've got to be kidding!" she shouted. "Just a minute. Hold on." She looked over at Tony. "Zarenko is on the move. The GPS shows them driving toward the hotel." Both she and Tony whipped their heads up to check the hotel entrance. Nothing so far. Tony immediately called Henri to let him know about Zarenko.

As Henri answered Tony's call, Katherine and Pauline exited the hotel and began walking down the driveway to the sidewalk.

"Henri, Zarenko's on the move. But look. Can you see them? The two women are coming toward us right now. Thank God."

Just when the two men were about to breathe a sigh of relief, a car swerved in front of the ladies and came to a stop at the end of the hotel driveway. The door opened and the men watched helplessly as Borovsky got out. He was waving his gun at the women. Then he took hold of Pauline's arm and pulled her toward the car. There was a maniacal look on his face. He shoved her in the back seat while he kept an eye on Katherine who was still standing there transfixed. He grabbed her and also shoved her into the back seat. After slamming the door, Ivan jumped in the front. The car sped away from the curb.

"Holy crap, what's happening," yelled Tony.

Edie opened her car door intending to go after them.

"Stay here. Stay here," Tony shouted. "We need to follow them. Did you see his gun? God, I hope he doesn't shoot them in the car. Son of a bitch, there goes my career right down the toilet." He started the car and tried to pull out into traffic, but it was morning rush hour. He had to wait for a numbers of cars to pass before he could proceed.

He was finally able to pull out into the heavy traffic. As soon as he had the chance, he was on the phone to Henri. "Where the hell are your people who were supposed to be guarding the women, Henri?" Tony yelled. "I thought you had a couple of guys in the hotel ready to follow them, for crying out loud."

Henri was as dumbfounded as Tony while he searched for his men. Right now all he saw were a bunch of tourists pouring out of the hotel door. Finally, he spotted the men exiting behind the group. They looked frantic. They ran down the driveway looking for the women. Henri pulled into traffic, drove up to the men, rolled down his window and flashed his badge. "Get in!" he shouted. The men barely had time to shut the doors before Henri went roaring down the street after Tony.

Edie was on her phone to the Embassy Duty Officer. She told him to keep her informed of Zarenko's whereabouts at all times. It was a good thing she had done that, because two blocks up, Borovsky's car shot through an intersection at the beginning of a red light. By the time Tony got there, he had no choice. He had to stop for the light.

Tony was on the phone to Henri. "Henri, it looks like Borovsky is heading for the warehouse. How many men do you have in place there?"

"There is only one man. I have just called him and told him to stay out of sight until we can get there."

Tony exploded. "What the hell? Why only one man covering that warehouse?" He was furious.

"You listen to me, Tony. Zarenko told us he thought Borovsky *might* bring the ladies to the warehouse. I don't have unlimited manpower here. So, yes, there is only one man at the warehouse. I have just contacted the Viennese police and told them to be ready to move once we know for sure where Borovsky is going. I have done the best I can, so you keep that temper of yours under control."

Henri's rebuke was like a bucket of cold water being thrown on him. It brought him back to his senses. Henri was right. He had to calm down. Screaming and yelling would solve nothing. "I apologize, Henri. I acted stupidly. Thanks."

He looked in his rearview mirror, but couldn't spot Henri's car. "Where are you? Can you see my car?"

"Yes. You are about four cars ahead of me. I was able to stop and pick up the two men from Interpol as they came out of the hotel. So they are with me now. Do whatever you have to do to get to Borovsky. I will follow you."

"Okay, good. Edie can keep in contact with the Embassy. They're monitoring Zarenko's GPS. I'll call again when I know for certain where they're going."

CHAPTER 33

The women were so stunned at what just happened, neither had time to react. Borovsky shoved Katherine into the car so hard she landed sideways on the edge of the seat and started to slide to the floor. Pauline caught her under the arms and helped her into a sitting position. Once she was upright, the two women looked at each other with fear in their eyes. They silently reached out and took each other's hand while giving each other the slightest nod. The gestures seemed to give them a modicum of strength.

As Katherine relaxed somewhat, she looked over at the man who was sitting in the back with them. He was on the other side of Pauline next to the window. "Hey, it's the guy from Amsterdam," she whispered.

In all the confusion, Pauline hadn't paid any attention to him. All of her concentration had been on

Katherine. But now she turned and took a good look at him. Katherine was right. It was the man she had helped in Holland.

Dimitri took Pauline's hand and gave it a quick squeeze while he cautiously glanced at Ivan in the front seat. She didn't know what to make of this. Was he doing this to let them know he was going to help them? Or was this a trick to get the diamonds back? She pulled her hand away and turned back to Katherine.

"So, I finally have you two," Borovsky said turning to his captives in the backseat. He had an evil smile on his face as he pointed his gun at them. Helmut was driving the car and flinched when Ivan waved his gun.

"Who are you?" Katherine asked in bewilderment.

"Do not play innocent with me," he responded. "You know that I am Ivan Borovsky." He continued to wave his gun at them. Katherine sucked in a quiet breath of air. Pauline dropped her head in resignation. Arthur's words about Borovsky being a very nasty man played in her mind.

In Russian Dimitri told Ivan shooting the ladies in the car would solve nothing, because they still did not know where the diamonds were. He urged him to get everyone to the warehouse. Ivan gave Dimitri a disgusted stare, but he did turn around and face the front.

With Ivan facing forward, Dimitri looked over at the ladies and put his index finger to his lips to indicate they should be quiet. He hoped the ladies would be smart enough to understand and keep their mouths shut. The least little thing could set Ivan off and make him uncontrollable.

After several turns and a long drive down a main street, Dimitri looked out the window. He realized it would only be a few more blocks until they reached the warehouse. He hoped the GPS watch was working. Did Henri and Tony know where they were and that Ivan now had the women? He hoped they did.

When they entered the warehouse parking lot, it was empty. No police cars anywhere. This worried him. His biggest problem now was going to be keeping Ivan from killing the women before help could arrive.

CHAPTER 34

As soon as the car stopped, Ivan was back to waving his gun again as he herded the women out of the car and through the warehouse door. Dimitri and Helmut followed the three into the building. Once inside, Ivan pointed to crates along the wall and told the women to sit down. Then he began to pace back and forth.

The two sat on the crates clutching their purses in front of them, almost like security blankets.

When they entered the warehouse, Helmut stood behind Ivan and Dimitri trying to look invisible. He had his arms wrapped around his waist and began rocking back and forth.

"Why have you done this to us?" Katherine demanded.

Dimitri winced. He knew it would be Katherine who would be the first one to speak.

Borovsky looked at her with a sneer on his face. "You know exactly why you are here. It was you two who sabotaged my mother in London. No one does that to my mother." He brought his gun up and waved it back and forth between the women.

"Sabotaged your mother?" she asked in a strong voice. "What are you talking about? We don't even know who your mother is."

Ivan was becoming more agitated. Pauline laid her hand on Katherine's arm trying to indicate she should be quiet.

"It was you who made the taxi break down in London," he screamed. "It was you who forced her to miss the train, so she could not get to Paris."

Katherine didn't get it. She just wouldn't shut up. "How could we make a taxi break down? We don't know the first thing about car engines."

Ivan rubbed his forehead. "You are lying," he screamed again. "You are trying to confuse me." His face showed pure rage. His hand shook as he pointed the gun directly at Katherine. "And now you will pay for what you have done. I am going to kill you, but slowly, bullet by bullet. And as you are dying, you will look in my eyes and know that nobody touches Ivan Brovosky's mother."

Ivan was no longer in touch with reality. He was obsessed about his mother. He hadn't even asked about the diamonds. They meant nothing to him. Dimitri was certain if he didn't act right now, Ivan really would begin shooting the women. Without waiting another second, he reached over, grabbed Ivan's wrist holding the gun and yanked his arm toward the ceiling. Thank goodness he didn't wait, because Ivan had pulled the trigger as his arm was going up. The roar of the gun was magnified in the confines of the warehouse. The bullet hit a light on the far wall. Shards of glass tinkled to the floor.

Before the glass finished falling, Ivan swung around and faced Dimitri. He began shouting at him in Russian. Neither woman understood what he was saying, but his body language left no doubt he would kill Dimitri for trying to save the women.

Even though Helmut had played computer war games since he was a young boy and even though he belonged to several violent, on-line commando clubs, he had never actually heard the sound of a real gun being fired. Seconds after Ivan's gun went off, his eyes rolled up into his head and he fell to the floor in a dead faint.

The thud of Helmut's body collapsing behind them distracted Ivan's tirade. Both he and Dimitri turned to see what had happened.

Without thinking, Pauline reached into her purse and grabbed the gun they had taken from Tony Cappelli. She remembered the safety was on. So while she pulled it out, she pushed the safety lever. Then she stood up, aimed in the general vicinity of Borovsky and pulled the trigger. She yelled "Enough!"

The recoil of the shot made the gun fly out of her hand. It skidded across the floor.

All the stars must have been aligned in the heavens when Pauline fired. Because when the bullet left her gun, even though Ivan and Dimitri were a mere 18 inches apart, it traveled straight toward Ivan. It hit him in the lower arm inches above his wrist shattering a small wrist bone. This caused his gun to fall out of his hand and onto the floor.

And then there was complete and utter silence.

When Pauline's gun exploded, Dimitri jerked back and was now staring at her in complete shock. Katherine stood with her jaw handing down as she looked at Pauline in total confusion. Ivan's arm was dangling at his side. He was fixated on the blood. It ran down the back of his hand and dripped off his two middle fingers. Pauline stood completely still staring down at her gun on the floor.

Pauline broke the silence. "Dear God," she whispered. She looked over at Katherine. "I shot another human being." Her face showed so much anguish. "Oh, my God, what have I done?" Tears rolled down her cheeks. Slowly, she started to walk toward Ivan. She had to help him.

Just then a horde of policemen with guns drawn exploded through the door of the warehouse shouting in English, Austrian and French. "Get down! Get down on the floor! Everyone get down now!"

Pauline didn't seem to hear them. She continued on the path toward Ivan. Katherine grabbed her and pulled her to her knees.

"Pauline, get down. We're safe now. See. Look at all the policemen," she shouted in Pauline's ear.

Pauline couldn't walk, so she started to crawl toward Ivan. "You don't understand. I have to help him," was all she said. Katherine didn't want her friend to be alone, so she crawled after her.

Tony spotted the gun Katherine had taken from him laying on the floor. He scooped it up and checked the safety. It was off. It must have been one of the guns that had been fired. An Austrian policeman saw Borovsky's gun on the floor next to him and grabbed it.

When the women reached Ivan, he was lying on the floor crying softly for his mother. "Moja Draga Mama, Moja Draga Mama," he kept muttering in Russian. Since the policemen had ceased shouting to get down, Katherine stood up next to Pauline who remained on her knees next to Ivan.

Tony and several others approached them. The policeman who had picked up Ivan's gun put his hands on Pauline's shoulders and tried to move her away.

She looked up at him. "No," she said. "I'm a nurse. I can help him."

She stayed where she was. She wanted to assess the damage of the bullet. As gently as she could, she pushed Ivan's coat sleeve up and unbuttoned his shirt cuff. She could see she needed to make a tourniquet to stop the bleeding, so she removed the scarf around her neck.

When she began tying it around Ivan's upper arm, the pain of the movement brought Ivan out of his trance. He looked up at Pauline and curled his lip. "You bitch. I'm going to kill you," he said between clenched teeth.

Katherine's eyes became tiny slits when she looked down at Ivan. "How dare he talk to my friend like that, she said. She looked at the group of people surrounding them. "The little pisser tried to kidnap us." Then she looked back at her friend who continued to help him. "Too bad, Pauline," she snarled. "You should have shot him in the mouth." With that, she brought her leg back intending to give Ivan a good, swift kick for what he had just said.

Fortunately, Tony saw what Katherine was about to do and yanked her away before she could make contact. He had no intention of letting her pull another kicking stunt.

"Don't you even think about it, Katherine," he hissed. "You come with me."

He continued to keep a firm grip on her arm as he led her over to the side.

When they got there, he spun her around and pushed her onto one of the crates. "You sit here and don't you move." His words were forceful. His face was mere inches from hers.

Katherine cocked her head in a haughty manner preparing to give him an indignant retort. But, when she looked up and saw the fury on his face, she thought better of it. But not to be outdone, she continued to look down her nose at him without saying a word.

Tony straightened, pointed a finger at her and told her one more time, "Don't you move."

With Katherine taken care of and out of the way, he went back to stay with Borovsky until the ambulance came.

He was impressed with Pauline. Throughout Ivan's ranting and raving, she continued to help him and monitor the bleeding. At one point, even Tony wanted to kick Ivan to shut him up. He could hear the siren of the approaching ambulance.

After Katherine smoothed her ruffled feathers, she realized sitting here wasn't so bad, because from this vantage point, she was able to watch everything going on in the whole warehouse. She also had time to think about how they were going to get out of this mess once and for all. A plan was developing. If anyone had been watching her, they would have seen one eyebrow go up and a slight smile form on her lips.

A few minutes later the only other woman in the warehouse, besides Katherine and Pauline, approached Katherine with her hand out.

"Hello, I'm Edie Patterson from the American Embassy here in Vienna. Are you Katherine or Pauline?"

"I'm Katherine."

After they shook hands, Edie sat down on the crate. "Can you tell me what happened?"

Katherine told her everything from the time Borovsky picked them up outside of the hotel up to the time Pauline fired the gun.

"I'm confused," Edie said. "I thought you were the one who took Tony's gun." She had a slight smile on her lips when she said that. "Why did Pauline have it?"

Katherine rolled her eyes in embarrassment. "Yes, I'm the one who took his gun, but I couldn't carry two guns in my purse. They were too heavy. See that man standing over there in handcuffs?" She pointed to Dimitri who was standing across the room. "I took his gun when we were in Amsterdam. So, I gave Tony's gun to Pauline to carry in her purse."

"Do you have the second gun with you now?" Edie asked.

"Yes, and I hate carrying it around," Katherine said.

Edie held out her hand. "Why don't you give it to me."

"Oh, thank goodness." Katherine was so relieved. She reached into her purse and pulled out Dimitri's gun. "Here. Take it," she said. But, before she could say another word, one of the Austrian policemen standing next to Helmut saw Katherine with the gun. He whipped out his gun and pointed it at her. With both hands holding the gun out in front of him and feet slightly apart, he assumed a defensive stance. Three other policemen saw what he had done and immediately responded accordingly. Now four policemen had their guns trained on Katherine.

Edie held up her hand to them and gently removed the gun from Katherine's hand. The policemen relaxed and holstered their guns.

"Oh, for crying-out-loud," Katherine said in exasperation. "You see what happens when you have a gun. You get more guns." She glared at the four officers.

"And besides, as if a little old lady like me could cause any trouble," she added.

Edie had to suppress a smile at Katherine's remark, since right now there were ten law enforcement people in the warehouse from three different agencies, all of whom were there because of this little old lady who *couldn't cause any trouble*. While she was enjoying her internal chuckle, she pressed a button on the gun, slid the cartridge of bullets out and put them in her coat pocket.

"Hey. How did you do that?" Katherine asked in surprise. "We wanted to take the guns apart so we could throw pieces of them away while we were traveling, but didn't know how to do that. Show me. Do it again."

"Ah, given the volatile situation here," Edie said nodding her head at the policemen, "I think another time would be better." She stood up, laid her hand on

Katherine's shoulder and leaned close to her. "Just to let you know," she whispered in her ear. "Taking Tony's gun in the manner you did, is going to provide a good story at the C.I.A. for years to come." She gave Katherine a wink before she turned to rejoin Tony and Henri.

The medics had arrived and had Ivan strapped on a stretcher. Men from Interpol and the Austrian police surrounded it as the medics wheeled Ivan out of the warehouse. Tony watched them leave. He allowed himself a smile and whispered, "Gotcha."

"He'll be well guarded at the hospital,' he said to Edie.

"Nice job," she replied.

With nothing left to do, Pauline walked over to Katherine and sat down to wait.

"Pauline, you should see how easy it is to remove the bullets from a gun. That lady over there took Dimitri's gun and slipped the bullets out just like that." She snapped her fingers for emphasis.

Pauline looked at Katherine and shook her head in sadness. "I don't ever want to have anything to do with guns again in my life."

Katherine put her arm around Pauline as the two sat quietly while they waited.

When they first entered the warehouse, Henri had pulled Dimitri aside and questioned him. Then he handcuffed him and handed him over to one of his Interpol colleagues. "Guard him," he said. "Do not let him out of your sight. I will be back as soon as I check on the other people."

He then walked over to Helmut who was now sitting up and conscious. After he asked him a few questions, Henri stood and made several calls on his cell phone.

Once Ivan and Helmut were escorted out of the warehouse, Henri walked back to where Dimitri was being detained.

"I will take over now," he told his colleague. When they were alone, Henri removed the handcuffs. He looked Dimitri in the eye. "Go," was all he said as he nodded his head toward the door.

"What?" Dimitri was dumbfounded.

"Get out of here before I change my mind."

Dimitri raised his arms slightly as he leaned toward Henri. His first impulse was to give him a big, Russian bear hug. But then he thought better of it, stopped and brought his arms back to his sides.

"You are serious. Why? Why are you doing this?"

Henri shrugged his shoulders before answering. "You helped us get to Borovsky, and you helped keep the women safe. So now you are free to go."

Dimitri nodded his head once and said "Thank you" before he turned to leave. As he walked away, thoughts began to speed through his mind. Now that Ivan is out, I can take over his business. First thing I need to do is get to Paris. I need to get my hands on Helmut's computers and retrieve all the information. As quickly as I can, I will hire another tech kid to help me transfer the money from Ivan's various accounts into mine. And then I will be in business. He looked like a cat who had just lapped up an entire dish of cream.

"Ah, Dimitri." Henri called out quietly behind him. Dimitri stopped in his tracks but didn't turn around. He kept his back to Henri. Just the sound of Henri's voice made him quite sure he was about to hear something he would not like.

"Just so you know, my men in Paris are on their way to Helmut's apartment as we speak to gather up all his computer equipment. And, by the way, all Ivan's bank accounts have been frozen."

Dimitri's head dropped. He pivoted slowly with his head down and a sheepish look on his face. When he raised his eyes and looked up at Henri, he doffed an imaginary hat. "A worthy opponent," he said to him. Henri, knowing what Dimitri was probably thinking, had a smirk on his face.

Dimitri turned once again and continued to the door. Ah, well. Perhaps this is a sign I should retire. Somewhere warm. Maybe one of the islands off the coast of Spain or Northern Africa.

CHAPTER 35

After Borovsky and Helmut had been carted off, Dimitri let go and all police business taken care of, Tony, Edie and Henri walked over to the women. Tony introduced Henri to the women. Then he said, "Come on. It's over. Now you will have to come to the Embassy, so we can debrief you."

Katherine stood up. "No, we don't want to go to the Embassy. We want you to take us back to our hotel. This has been a horrible experience. I need to help my friend. I can't do it if we're sitting in a cold, bare room at the Embassy." Having them taken back to the hotel was part of the plan she had devised while she was sitting on the crate.

"There are no cold, bare rooms in the Embassy," Edie said with a smile. "You'll be very comfortable. In fact, we'll even bring you coffee and a light meal."

"No. I want you to take us back to our hotel. This has been an ordeal. I'm very concerned about my friend." She put her hand on Pauline's shoulder. "We've been through enough. We need time. We're just two old ladies you know."

Tony rolled his eyes at that one.

Then he squinted at Katherine with a skeptical look on his face as if to say, she's up to something. He had been in the espionage game for a long time. Old ladies or hardened criminals, he knew subterfuge when he heard it.

Right now Pauline was exhausted and wanted to be away from here. "Look, Katherine's right. We need a quiet place to calm down. And we need to contact our children to let them know we're finally safe." She glared at Tony. "Don't forget it was you who ordered the FBI go to our children's homes and scare them about all this. Now, quit arguing and just take us back to our hotel."

"I think they're right Tony," Edie said. "Give them a few hours. We can bring them over later this afternoon."

"I agree," Henri chimed in giving Tony a how could you be so insensitive look.

Tony did not respond to any of them. All his training in counter-intelligence had kicked up a notch. So far the diamonds hadn't appeared. A half hour ago, Henri arranged to have the women's hotel room searched. The Austrian police did not find any trace of the diamonds. The natural instinct in him caused alarm bells to go off.

"All right, you can go back to the hotel, but Henri and I are going with you. You can have your time, but then I have some questions you need to answer. You can answer them just as easily in your room as the Embassy."

Not quite what Katherine had in mind, but it was a start. She needed to get Pauline alone to tell her about her plan. However, with Tony and Henri in the hotel room, it was going to be difficult.

Pauline had come to the end of her patience, "I've had enough. I want to get out of here. Please take us to our hotel." Tears started to run down her cheeks. Pauline's tears gave Katherine an idea.

On their way out of the warehouse, she took Pauline's arm and slowed her down, putting a small distance between them and the other three.

"When I give you the signal in our room, I want you to start crying," Katherine whispered.

"Oh, come on," Pauline said. There was such weariness in her whole demeanor. "I can't put up with any more of your schemes right now. Not now, Katherine." She felt defeated by all that had happened.

Katherine gave her friend a slight shake. "Hey, buck up, Pauline," she said quietly. "You were a hero today. Don't you realize it was you who saved us from getting killed, for heaven's sakes? You did that."

Pauline was silent for a few beats while she processed what Katherine said. The forlorn look slowly ebbed from her face somewhat. Her shoulders seemed to straighten a bit as her chin rose slightly. "I did, didn't I?" she whispered with a tiny, sad smile playing across her face.

CHAPTER 36

The ride back to the hotel was quiet. The four of them were each lost in their private thoughts.

Pauline was wondering whether she would ever get over the fact she had shot someone. Even though Borovsky was a horrible man, it did not play into the equation of her grief. Katherine's pep talk helped somewhat. But the bottom line still was – she had shot another human being.

Henri was glad this was over and the women were finally safe. Over the weeks, he had come to admire the ladies. With all that happened to them, they seemed to have remained strong.

Ever the pessimist, Tony kept waiting for the other shoe to drop. Something else is going to go wrong. This is not the end. The big question is where are the diamonds?

I want to go home was paramount on Katherine's mind. *How can we get home safely? I think my plan will work.*

When they got to the hotel room, Tony took their key card and opened the door. He and Henri entered first and did a cursory check of the room before the women were allowed to enter.

Pauline stood at the door for a moment. She shook her head back and forth silently and closed her eyes trying to shake off the horror of the day. Then she walked in and sat down on the bed next to Katherine. Tony and Henri took the two chairs in front of the window.

"First, I want to apologize to you both. This wasn't supposed to happen." Katherine and Pauline snorted and gave Tony a *yeah-right* look. He could understand their reaction, but he also wanted them to know how hard they had worked trying to keep them safe.

"Last night we assigned a two-men team from Interpol inside your hotel to watch you round the clock. When you left this morning they were to follow you to the Embassy. Edie and I were in a car parked one block away from the hotel and Henri", he swung his arm out in Henri's direction, "was parked right behind me. So you were well covered. But, when you came out of the hotel, you two managed to leave in front of the large group of tourists.

Unfortunately, the men from Interpol were behind the group and couldn't get past them in time to exit with you."

"Oh, by the way, which one of you charged something this morning?" Tony asked.

Pauline had an embarrassed look on her face when she raised her hand. "I did. It was a crystal clown."

Tony had a look of confusion on his face while he was processing a *crystal clown*. "Well, that's how Borovsky found out where you were. He was monitoring your credit cards. When you made the purchase this morning, Pauline, he was able to zero in on you."

"Good grief," Katherine said. "You mean to tell me, people can get into our credit card accounts and do things like that?"

"Remember the young man who fainted in the warehouse? He's Ivan's techie whiz kid who hacked into your accounts. Just to let you know, even we have been following you since Paris through your credit card purchases and your cell phone activity."

"How awful," Pauline said. "We have no privacy at all, do we?"

Tony gave a rueful smile. "Not any more, I'm afraid."

Then Tony asked an unexpected question. "Which one of you has friends at the State Department in Washington?"

"State Department?" Pauline said and shrugged her shoulders. "Not me. Well, other than my friend who's daughter works at the Embassy in Rome." She turned to Katherine. "Remember? I told you about her. How about you? Do you know anyone who works there?"

Katherine shook her head and looked completely baffled when she turned back to Tony. "Why are you asking us about the State Department?"

"Yesterday, a Mr. Robertson at the State Department called the Embassy in Vienna to inquire about the two of you. Does the name ring a bell?"

"Nope," they both answered in unison and shook their heads.

Pauline snapped her fingers. "Wait a minute," she said to Katherine. "I wonder if it has something to do with Arthur."

"Oh, of course, Arthur," Katherine said.

"Who's Arthur," Tony asked.

"He's my attorney," Katherine said.

"He's her friend," Pauline smiled.

"My attorney." Katherine gave Pauline a menacing look.

"Her friend." Pauline wiggled her eyebrows and smirked. She didn't seem intimidated by Katherine's look at all.

Katherine sliced her hand through the air to end the discussion of just who Arthur was.

She turned to Tony. "We talked to Arthur a few days ago and told him we didn't know what was happening to us. He said he was going to contact one of his old college friends who used to work in Washington at the State Department to find out what was going on. His friend must still have some pull, and that's why you got the phone call."

Tony nodded his head but said nothing for a minute. "So Arthur, an attorney slash friend, in Wisconsin was able to pull those strings?"

"Well, for all intents and purposes, he's a retired attorney," Katherine answered. "But, since his name is the first one on the door, he still keeps a few clients."

"Interesting," Tony said. It answered the question of how he got the phone call from Washington.

He waited a moment then he raised his eyebrows and cocked his head at the two. "All right, ladies." He gave out a sigh. "We are going to have to talk about what happened during your ordeal. Pauline? Are you up for this?" he asked.

Pauline just nodded her head in resignation.

Katherine stood up quickly. "Wait a minute. Hold it," she said. "This has been the worst day of our lives."

She slowly shook her head back and forth. "We're not ready to relive this yet. Pauline and I have been friends for over fifty-five years. I want you two to leave the room and give us some time to be alone. And, then we need to call our children. They need to know we're safe. Why don't you go down and grab a cup of coffee?"

"Of course," Henri answered immediately. He understood the ordeal they had been through and their need for privacy. He rose and started for the door.

Tony stood up but did not move. He was in his espionage mode of *trust no one*. He glared at the women without saying a word. His lips were pressed together with a slight snarl indicating distrust. He scanned the room looking for escape routes.

First he walked over to the window and looked down. He looked back at the bed calculating whether they could tie the sheets together to escape through the window. It was a straight drop of four floors. The sheets wouldn't get them passed the third floor, so that was out.

Next, he scanned the interior of room and spotted the return-air duct high in the wall above the beds. He grabbed the desk chair and dragged it over the duct.

Henri was stunned when Tony climbed on the chair. "Tony, what are you doing?" he asked.

The women just sat there with confusion written on their faces as they followed Tony's movements.

"I just want to check this air duct," he answered. He peered through the slats of the vent cover and could see the duct was too small for either of them to crawl through to make a get-away.

He returned the chair to the desk and turned to the women. "I want one of your room keycards. I want to have access to this room. Henri and I will be right outside the door."

Katherine took the keycard from her pocket and handed it to Tony. "What brought this on? You're treating us like we're the enemy. I'll bet Borovsky is being treated better than we are right now. And, that idiot is an arms dealer and a murderer for crying out loud."

Henri had had enough. He seemed embarrassed by Tony's behavior and took him by the arm and escorted him to the door. Once they were in the hall and the door was shut, he confronted Tony.

"You want to tell me what that was all about. Katherine was right. You treated them as if they were the enemy. After all those two have been through, you embarrassed me with your behavior.

"Henri, those two are up to something. I don't know what it is, but I'm sure it has to do with the diamonds."

Henri threw up his hands in disgust. "Let them have some peace. We searched their room and did not find them, so I am sure they are carrying them on their person probably in their purses. You will see. When we go back in, they will reach in and hand the diamonds over to us."

The way this day was going, he just looked over at Henri and snorted.

CHAPTER 37

When the men left the room, Katherine walked to the door. She checked it to make sure they had actually shut it completely. They had.

She went back to the bed and sat down next to Pauline and took her hand. "Listen," she said to her friend. "I want to go home. Honest to goodness, Pauline, I have never been so frightened in my life. I thought Borovsky was going to kill us this morning. Remember when I told you I wanted to live until I went in a ditch? I didn't care when that was? Yeah well, I lied. This morning I made up my mind. I want to live until I'm eighty like you." She gave Pauline a sad smile.

Pauline's lower lip began to quiver. "Oh God, Katherine. I'm still scared too. Did you hear all the threats Borovsky kept making while I was taking care of his arm? What are we going to do?" With that, she began to cry as she grabbed Katherine.

Katherine hugged her tightly. She had to swallow a number of times to keep from loosing control, but finally even she couldn't stop the tears. The two of them sat there and sobbed uncontrollably.

After a short time of wiping away tears with their hands and then with their sleeves, both took a tissue from their purses. They blew their noses in unison, looked at each other and started to laugh sadly.

"What a mess we're in," Pauline said shaking her head. She took another tissue and wiped her face.

"Whew. I think the cry did us a world of good," Katherine said. She took Pauline's hand again. "Now listen. I'm still scared too. And, I did hear the way Borovsky kept threatening you before they took him away. How do we know he's not making phone calls right now in the hospital arranging for people to kill us?"

Pauline covered her face with her hands. She seemed to collapse within herself. "Oh, no. Do you really think so?"

"I don't know. But when I was sitting in the warehouse, I started thinking."

Pauline looked like she was about to protest. Katherine held up her hand. "Just hear me out. I think these diamonds are going to be our ticket for getting us home," she said while pointing back and forth between their boobs.

"The way I figure it is if we just hand them over right now, we're done. Everyone will say '*thanks a lot and see ya*'. Then we'll be on our own as the door closes behind us. I don't want to go home alone. I don't want to take a chance on anything that idiot, Borovsky, might do. That's all we need. Now instead of him, there's a good chance we could be running around trying to get away from the assassins he hired. Only now we'd be all alone. No good guys chasing us too, ready to help."

Pauline lip started to quiver again.

"Oh no, you don't," Katherine said harshly. "Don't you start to cry again. I need you to focus. We need to plan this out."

Pauline faced forward and took a deep breath and blew it out slowly. She turned to Katherine. "Okay. What's the plan, oh great one?"

Katherine smiled. "You know how the CIA have those little planes they use to fly people around? Well, I want the CIA to fly us home in one of them. And, we should be able to get them to do it by using the diamonds as our bargaining chip."

"What are you talking about?" Pauline asked. She had a bewildered look on her face. "You just said once we turn over the diamonds, they won't help us anymore."

"Aha! That's just it. Suppose we don't turn over the diamonds? We tell them we mailed them to a friend in the States. And, we won't tell them where we mailed them unless they agree to fly us home."

"But we didn't mail them. We still have them," Pauline said hefting her boobs.

"I know that and you know that, but they don't know that. Don't' you see, we have to have a reason for them to fly us home. I think the diamonds are our ace in the hole."

Pauline stood up and walked to the window. "You really think it would work?" she asked quietly looking out at the skyline of Vienna. "Personally, I don't think the diamonds are important to them now that they have Borovsky?"

"Good heavens, Pauline. We have a million dollars in diamonds stashed in our bras. So, yes, I think they're very important. Oh, and one more thing. We can't let them take us to the Embassy. If we go there, we have to walk through some sort of security monitor. I'm not sure, but I bet the diamonds would show up on their scanners if we did that."

"And, you did all this thinking while you were sitting there in the warehouse this morning?" Pauline asked while she continued to stare out the window.

"Yeah. It started when I thought about how scared I was and how I wanted everything to end – no more chasing, no more bad guys, no more guns. And that led to how do we get out of this mess? And just then, I had to scratch one of my boobs, because a diamond was bugging me. And, I thought, aha!" Katherine shrugged her shoulders as if to say, that's how it happened.

Pauline remained quiet and continued to stare out the window. A small smile played across her face as she continued to study the city. After a while she said, "Well, I can't think of anything better. So I guess it's worth a try, isn't it?" She turned back and gave Katherine a helpless gesture.

"Before we call Mutt and Jeff back in here, I want to phone my children," Katherine said. She began digging in her purse to get to her cell phone. "They should know we're safe and that it's all over. I don't know what time it is in Wisconsin right now. But to tell you the truth, I don't really care if I wake them up out of a sound sleep or not. I just need to hear their voices."

She stopped for a moment. "But no way am I telling them everything. If I do, they'll be nagging me for months. I'll be put on the family watch list. I'll probably have to call them for permission just to go to the grocery store. And let's not tell the kids our plans to be flown home either. If we tell them what we're trying to do, we're going to have to explain what happened in the warehouse and the threats Bovorsky made. It will just upset them."

Pauline was nodding her head. "You're right. We'll be vague about this morning." There was a twinkle in her eyes as she wiggled her eyebrows. "Actually, we can look at this as payback time for their high school years when they didn't tell us everything either."

"You got that right," Katherine chuckled.

Pauline walked from the window and sat on the opposite bed, leaned back on the pillow and put her arm over her forehead. "You make your calls first. I just need to relax before I make mine. And the one thing I can't do is phone Dennis. I'll ask Rosie to call him and tell him I'm okay. After all that's happened to us this morning, I'm not ready to handle any of his tirades right now." She closed her eyes and added, "What kind of mother am I who won't call her own son?" She sounded so weary.

"You know, Pauline, there comes a time when we mothers have to stop feeling responsible for our children's behavior. They're adults. They have to answer for themselves. Dennis made his choices. His negativity is something he chose, and he has to answer for it, not you. Don't add needless guilt to everything else that's happened to us today."

Katherine pressed speed dial on her phone for Bernie's number. She was right about the time difference. Because of the seven-hour difference, she woke him and each of the other children when she called.

"Hello, Bernie? It's Mom. I'm calling to tell you everything is over and Pauline and I are safe."

"Yeah, the American Embassy told us the police caught the Russian guy this morning." She looked over at Pauline and wiggled her eyebrows.

"No, we're at our hotel in Vienna right now."

"Right. The bottom line is we're safe and it's over."

She chuckled as she listened to her son. "Yup, we've decided to come home too. We've had enough adventure for a while. But I have to call you back about our return flight information. Everything happened so fast this morning we haven't had time to make any arrangements.

"I'll call as soon as I know when we'll be coming home. Right, I love you too, honey. Bye, see you soon." She had to blink a few times as she hung up, because she got misty eyed hearing her sons voice.

"Okay. Now I have to call Priscilla. Sons are so easy. They're very pragmatic. You have a problem? Is it solved? Good, done, nothing more to say. But Priscilla, being female, will grill me. I'll probably have to lie through my teeth to get through the call with her," she said while she brought up her number.

"Hi, Priscilla, I'm sorry to wake you, but I want to let you know Pauline and I are safe now. The American Embassy said the police caught the Russian guy this morning."

"No, I don't know too much about it. They just said they got him in some warehouse here in Vienna. That's all we know." She looked over at Pauline and made a face.

"Gun? What gun? Oh, the one we mentioned on that phone call with the FBI. Yeah, right. It was nothing. Pauline and I found it in some bushes and didn't want to dispose of it along the road. We felt someone might find it and be able to use it, so we kept it. But I turned it over to a woman at the Embassy this morning. So that's over."

"Diamonds?" She rolled her eyes at her friend. "Now that's a funny story." Even Pauline could hear Priscilla shouting at her mother.

"Hold on, hold on. Let me tell you about it. See the guy in Paris . . ."

"Well, he was a gun buyer from Africa." This time she held the phone away from her ear as Priscilla exploded.

"Priscilla, Honey, stop and just listen, because it really is a funny story. The man in Paris gave us the diamonds thinking we were the Russian guy's mother and aunt. Then he walked away. We didn't have time to give them back. We didn't know what to do, so get this. We stuffed the diamonds in our bras. Isn't that funny. We've been running around Europe all this time with the diamonds in our bras." There was absolutely no laughter on Priscilla's end. But she wasn't finished with her questions for her mother.

"The Russian guy? I thought you knew. He's an arms dealer here in Europe."

"No, no, no. We never met the guy." She looked at Pauline and crossed her fingers. "And, remember, I told you he was caught this morning."

"What do you mean, how did we know he was chasing us?" She waited a heartbeat before responding. "Well, we, ah, assumed he was. We had the diamonds appraised in Antwerp and knew they were worth about a million dollars. Everything seemed odd. And, and, getting the phone calls with all you kids and the FBI gave us a clue."

"Well, the reason we stayed in Europe was because we didn't know what was going on. And we still hadn't seen all of the things we planned to see."

"Of course, I'm telling you everything." She looked at Pauline and crossed her eyes on that one.

"Well, look. I still have to call Jane and let her know, I'm okay and Pauline has to call her kids. Oh, and we're coming home, but haven't had time to make our flight reservations yet. They just caught the guy this morning. So, I'll call you back when I know our flight times."

"Yeah, right. I'm glad we're all right too and I love you too, Honey. Bye, love."

"Whew. I knew she'd do that to me," Katherine said when she hung up.

"She takes after you, you know?" Pauline chuckled.

The phone call with Jane was easy, because as soon as Jane heard her mother's voice, she started to cry. So all Katherine had to do was tell her she was safe and would call her later with the flight information.

Pauline then called her daughter, Rosie. It, too, was an easy call. Pauline told her they were safe. Borovsky had been captured. They turned the gun over to the Embassy and the diamonds would be taken care of this afternoon. Rosie was so glad to hear her mother's voice, she didn't ask too many questions, but she did want to know when was Pauline coming home. She also told Pauline not to worry, she understood completely. She would call Dennis.

"Well, I suppose I should call Arthur and let him know it's all over," Katherine said after the final call to kids.

"Of course, you should call him," Pauline said. "After all, he worked hard to find out what was going on with us. You owe him that. And didn't he say to call him anytime once we were safe?"

"Yeah, you're right." She proceeded to punch in his phone number.

"Hello, Arthur? It's Katherine. We're safe. It's all over."

"Oh, thank goodness," Arthur said. "Where are you now? At the Embassy?"

"We're in Vienna and I'm calling from our hotel room. I'm going to tell you what happened, but you can't tell the kids. Okay?" Katherine asked.

"Oh dear. This doesn't sound good. But you are safe and it's all over? Right?"

"Yes, yes, we're fine and safe. But this morning Borovsky kidnapped us, took us to a warehouse and was going to kill us." Katherine said.

"What?" Arthur said. "I don't believe what I'm hearing, Katherine.

"But everything is fine now, because Pauline shot him." Katherine looked over at her friend. Pauline just closed her eyes and dropped her head. The sadness seemed to return.

"Pauline shot him?" Arthur asked in surprise. After a few beats, he said, "All right, Katherine. Start at the beginning and tell me every thing that happened."

And she did. "And now we're scared. We want to come home, but we're afraid to travel by ourselves in case there are other people sent to kill us. So we're going to ask Tony, that's the CIA guy, to fly us home in one of the CIA's private planes. I'm not sure he'll agree to it, so we're going to tell him we won't tell him where the diamonds are unless he agrees."

Arthur chuckled quietly. "Well, if anyone can pull it off, it's you, my dear."

"Please don't tell our kids about our being kidnapped. They don't need to know about that," Katherine said. "And whatever you do, don't tell anyone about Pauline shooting Borovsky. She's very upset about it. And if our kids hear that, they'll put us in quarantine for life. We won't be able to go anywhere."

"No, of course not. I understand. When do you think you'll be coming home?"

"We plan to make our request this morning."

"Call me and let me know when you'll be home," Arthur said.

"Yes," Katherine answered. "And thank you for all your help. You really helped us, Arthur. Now you can go back to sleep."

"Afraid not. At my age, once you're up you're up."

When they were through with their calls, Katherine went to the door. Tony and Henri were waiting in the hall.

CHAPTER 38

Once the four of them were seated again, Katherine and Pauline together on the bed, Tony and Henri in the chairs, it was Katherine who broke the silence.

"All right, we're ready to answer your questions now."

"Did you call your children?" Tony asked.

"Yes," Pauline smiled. "We woke them up. It's only five o'clock over there, but they were glad to hear we're safe."

"Okay, good. Now I need you to start at the beginning. I want you two to tell us what happened to you and where you've been. We need to compare notes and make sure we're in agreement. We know you were mistaken for Borovsky's mother and aunt when you were on the Eurostar. And the man following you gave you the diamonds by mistake when you were in Paris.

"So then you left Paris and drove to Amsterdam making a stop in Antwerp, right?"

"How do you know we stopped in Antwerp?" Katherine was taken by surprise that Tony even knew that.

It was Henri who answered. "The jeweler reported your names and license plate number to Interpol. Apparently, he didn't believe whatever story you gave him."

"That Narc," Katherine said in disgust. She heard her grandson say that. Tony looked amused.

"So in Amsterdam you met Dimitri Zarenko and picked up your first gun," Tony said looking at them with a raised eyebrow.

"Actually, Katherine took his gun when he went into shock after being stung by a bee. I have the same problem. I always carry medicine with me in case I'm stung. That's why I was able to help Dimitri with my medicine. I told Katherine to go get help. Before she left she took the gun to protect me. She didn't know if Dimitri would come around and use his gun on me while she was looking for help."

Katherine looked at Pauline and smiled. "Thanks. I'm glad you finally understand why I did it." Pauline patted her hand.

"Then you left and went where?"

"Well, first we drove to Koblenz and tried to ditch the gun in the Rhine River. But there were always too many people near us. So we decided to come here to Vienna figuring Vienna would probably have the biggest American Embassy to help us. But we wanted to go to Zurich before driving here. Neither of us had ever been in Switzerland and other than the one encounter with Dimitri, we had no idea everyone was following us." Katherine said.

"I want to tell you things you may not know," Tony said with a smile. "I believe you two were standing right behind me at a stop light in Paris. Looking back on it, I'm quite sure you had just received the diamonds. One of you said *that was weird* and *is it heavy*. I was on my way to the George Cinq. We heard Borovsky's mother was coming there. Standing at the stoplight, I remember your accents mostly. Pure Midwest, by the way," Tony smiled. The women groaned when they heard that. "And then I heard you again as you passed us on your way to dinner in the hotel. Henri and I were both sitting there in the lobby."

"So in other words, it could have all been over the first day had we only known who each other was?" Pauline asked.

Tony nodded sadly. "Here's another one. When you were in Zurich, all four of us were there looking for you, Henri and I, Borovsky, and Dimitri. Because the street monitors weren't working at the outskirts of the city, as soon as you entered Zurich all of us lost you. Other than your hotel bill, you never charged anything, did you? So none of us could trace your whereabouts that way either."

"We decided to use our Euros in Zurich," Katherine said. "We were trying to act like normal tourists. That's why we came to Europe in the first place."

"Did you know Borovsky followed you to the cable car park in Lichtenstein?" Tony asked.

Both women said, "No," at the same time.

Pauline turned to Katherine. "I didn't see him, did you?"

Katherine was so amazed at what Tony had said. "Good grief. This is like the Keystone Kops for heaven's sakes," she said. "We thought we were all alone. So all this time the good guys," she opened her hand to the two men. "And the bad guys were all near one another. But we didn't know it."

But then she stopped and looked at Tony for a moment. "Why didn't you arrest Borovsky right there at the cable car place?" she asked softly. "Why did you let him go?"

Tony blew out a breath of air. "We couldn't arrest him in Lichtenstein. We had nothing to charge him with. At that point, he hadn't committed any crime."

"Soooo . . . in other words, you *wanted* him to kidnap us. Is that it?" she asked.

"At first, yes," he nodded his head slowly. "But when I thought it through, I couldn't let him go through with it. That's why we all came to the hotel this morning. But then things went wrong. I'm sorry."

Henri waited a few beats and then reached into his inside pocket. "I have a picture I want you to look at." He pulled it out and handed it to Katherine. It wiped the smile off the women's faces. The picture of the African buyer had been taken at the morgue.

"Is this the man who gave you the diamonds at the café in Paris?" he asked. "I am sorry. This is the only photo we have. The gentleman was killed the day after he gave you the diamonds."

Both Katherine and Pauline sucked in air when they saw it and looked away. The reality of looking at the morgue picture was more than they ever experienced. Even Pauline with her medical background was affected by what she saw.

"In Amsterdam Dimitri told us he had the man killed," Pauline said softly. "We didn't know if it was the truth or he was just trying to scare us." She handed the picture back to Henri.

"So this is definitely the man who gave you the diamonds in Paris?" Henri asked.

They both nodded and whispered, "Yes."

He put the picture back in his pocket and said, "I can see you feel responsible for this gentleman's death. I want you to know, you are not. He made the mistake. He was an arms broker for many years and was fully aware of the dangers of his profession. It was Borovsky who ordered the hit. I assure you, you two had absolutely nothing to do with his death. You were merely in the wrong place at the wrong time."

Tony looked at the two women and spoke quietly. "And now we come to the diamonds." He waited a moment and then asked, "Where are they?"

Pauline turned to Katherine and whispered, "You're on," meaning she had the stage all to herself.

Katherine cleared her throat with a brief cough. "We don't have the diamonds anymore. We mailed them to the United States, and . . ."

She didn't get a chance to finish her sentence, because Tony jumped up and started shouting, "I knew it. I knew they were up to something, Henri. I told you. I told you they would do something like this."

"Sit . . . down . . . Tony." Katherine raised her voice and emphasized each word separately. Then she used the big one. She gave him a *mother look*.

His jaw dropped. He literally had to take a step back. That look was just like the one his mother used to give him when he was a teenager.

"What the hell," he said to no one in particular. "Do all mothers go to mother's school to learn that look?" But he did sit down.

"Now," Katherine continued. "Pauline and I are very scared. We've never been involved in anything like this. Guns, arms dealers, chases, having our lives threatened and seeing a picture of someone murdered." She pointed to Henri.

"No, we're more than scared. We are terrified. You heard Borovsky making all those threats to Pauline this morning. We're afraid if we tell you where the diamonds are, you'll just take them, walk away, and leave us to find our own way home. And because of Borovsky, there could still be more men chasing us. Only this time there will be no one to help us. So I have a plan."

Tony snorted. "Oh, brother," he said.

Henri was smiling in admiration as he waited to hear the plan.

"We sent the diamonds to a friend of ours in the U.S. with instructions to keep them until we got home. So here's the deal, we want you to fly us home in one of those CIA planes. And, when we're out over the Atlantic, we'll tell you where we mailed the diamonds." She smiled and looked at the two men waiting for their answer.

"No way," Tony said emphatically. "It would cost tens of thousands of dollars to arrange for a private plane to fly you two home. Tell us where the diamonds are and we'll see to it you're escorted directly to the door of a commercial plane which can then take you home."

"Can you guarantee Borovsky won't have men on the plane following us, waiting for their chance to kill us?" It was Pauline who asked the question. "You just told us about all the times you were this close to us." She held up her finger and thumb about an inch apart. "But all those times, you couldn't protect us. Borovsky still kidnapped us. I'm sorry, Tony, but we want to fly home in a special CIA plane. We don't want to be alone."

Tony stood up. "I'm sorry, ladies. But escorting you to your own plane is the best I can do. Now where are the diamonds?"

Katherine and Pauline pursed their lips together and looked up at the ceiling. Their message was simple. We are not going to tell you.

"I could have you arrested, you know?" Tony growled at them.

"No you can't," Katherine said. "You don't have the authority."

"Maybe not, but here's what I can do. I'm going back to the Embassy and revoke your passports. You won't be able to leave the country. If you even try to venture out of this room, I'll see to it the Viennese police know about it. And since neither of you will have a valid passport, you *will* be arrested on the spot and put in jail. Chew on that one, ladies."

Pauline looked at Tony and smiled. "You won't do that."

"Don't count on it, Pauline. You have no idea how ruthless I can be."

Pauline remained smiling and slowly shook her head. "You won't do that, because you're too nice."

Tony threw up his hands. "You women are driving me nuts," he said in frustration. He looked over at Henri. "Well, if they handled Borovsky this morning, I must look like a pussycat with my threats."

Henri gave Tony a benign smile but said nothing. His demeanor seemed clear. You got yourself into this. You can get yourself out of it.

Katherine rose. "Gentlemen, that's our offer. You fly us home in one of your jet planes, so we can feel safe. And we'll keep our end of the bargain and tell you where the diamonds are."

Tony wanted to choke her. "Then you can sit here in this room until you tell us where the diamonds are. Once you do that, we'll escort you to your commercial plane. No way am I going to commandeer a CIA plane just to get the diamonds back. And, that's my final offer. Come on, Henri, let's go."

Pauline stood and walked over to Henri. "Do you think you could have those two Interpol men stay here at the hotel? And, would you mind pointing them out to us. If we want to leave the hotel, we'll be sure to wait for them to follow us." She spoke to Henri as if Tony's threats meant nothing. "We wouldn't want them to get stuck behind a group of tourist like they did this morning."

"They are in the lobby right now. Come. I will introduce you," Henri said and offered Pauline his arm.

When they returned after their introduction to the men from Interpol, Katherine made one phone call. She called Arthur.

CHAPTER 39

Back at the Embassy Tony was pacing back and forth in Edie's office while he ranted and raved. "Can you believe it? They expect us to fly them home in one of our planes, for god's sake. I tell you those two women are making me crazy. They're fearless. I threaten them and they smile at me, for crying out loud."

"Well, they've been through some scary things for civilians. What do you expect, Tony? I can understand how frightened they must be," Edie said.

"I offered to take them right to the door of their plane," he shouted while waving his arm in the air imitating a plane taking off.

"I'll tell you, Edie, those women are sneaky and conniving."

"Oh, come on, Tony," Edie said with a chuckle. "You're just angry because those two have you over a barrel on this one."

Tony stopped his pacing and swung around and glared at Edie. "Don't you dare try to bring humor into this. There is absolutely nothing funny about it. It wasn't just me. Those two threatened the CIA for crying out loud."

Tony's anger and frustration were evident. Edie stopped smiling. "You're right. I won't make light of this again. But, honest to goodness, Tony, I sat with Katherine in the warehouse. And then I watched as Pauline took care of Borovsky. There's nothing *sneaky or conniving* about either one of them. They're just two, nice, old ladies who got themselves into a very bad situation by accident. And thank goodness, they made it through alive and well."

"Oh, that's what you think – *nice old ladies*," Tony said with a sneer on his lips. "You weren't in the hotel room this morning with their planning and scheming. You know what Katherine did right before we left the hotel? She winked at Henri and told him if he were a few years younger, she would chase him around the Eiffel Tower. And Henri, that aging Lothario, winked right back and said 'If I were a few years younger, I would let you catch me.'"

Edie put her hand over her mouth to stifle the laughter on that one. She knew how upset Tony was. However, before she could say anymore, the phone on her desk rang. The light indicated it was her secretary in the outer office.

"Yup, Marge. What's up?" she said when she picked up the phone.

"Yes, he's here. Okay, I'll get him."

"You have an incoming call from Washington." Edie held the phone out to Tony. "Here, Marge will patch you through."

Tony rolled his eyes and grabbed the phone from Edie's hand. "Now what? This day can't get any worse."

"Hello, this is Tony Cappelli," he said in a crisp, no nonsense voice. Then his jaw dropped open, his eyebrows shot up and his eyes got huge.

"Good morning to you too, Sir."

"Yes, Sir, the ladies are safe. Interpol has two men stationed in their hotel."

"Well, we're waiting for them to tell us where the diamonds are, Sir."

"No, Sir, we are not holding them hostage."

"No, Sir. I have not revoked their passports, Sir. I just tried to use that as a bargaining chip to get them to tell us where the diamonds are."

"I do understand they've been through a lot."

"Well, I don't know if I would describe them as *helpless* old ladies, Sir."

"No, Sir. I'm not being facetious. It's just I don't think they're as helpless as you might think."

"Yes, Sir. They did say if we fly them home in one of our planes, they would tell us where the diamonds are."

"Yes, Sir. I understand. I'll requisition the plane as soon as I get off this call."

"No, Sir. Right, you won't be bothered by this again."

"You have a good day too, Sir."

Tony slowly hung up the phone. He remained standing facing the outside window. "That was the Director of the whole fricken Central Intelligence Agency," he said very softly.

Edie was flabbergasted. The Director of Central Intelligence was only one step away from the President. No jokes now.

"What did the DCI want?" she asked incredulously.

Very slowly, he turned toward Edie. He worked hard to keep his composure. "He ordered me to fly Katherine and Pauline home in one of our planes." There was intense anger on his face. Both hands at his sides were balled into fists.

"Oh, my God," Edie said. "How did that happen?"

"I have no idea." The words came out slowly. Tony never felt so utterly close to losing his sanity. Over the course of his career, he had gone toe-to-toe with terrorists, hardened criminals, and spies. He always kept his cool, kept himself in control in each and every situation. Yet within a matter of minutes he was brought to his knees by two, wacky, old ladies who thought he was nice. He couldn't believe it.

Edie saw pure rage and confusion on his face. She needed to get him focused and back to reality again. Very calmly she walked to the door of her office. Opening it, she said, "Well, I think you should go down to the secure room and make the arrangements. Don't you?"

Tony seemed to come out of his trance. He gave his head a little shake. "Yeah, you're right. I'll go make the arrangements. Edie, how the hell did those two manage to get the Director of the entire frickin Agency involved?" He looked at her in total disbelief.

As soon as Tony exited, Edie quickly closed the door, because amusement started to bubble up inside of her. When Tony got to the end of the hall, he heard an explosion of laughter coming from her office. He got angry all over again and stormed off.

CHAPTER 40

The next morning when Pauline opened the door to their hotel room, she found Tony standing there. He didn't move. He was like a statue. He just stared at her. Through clenched teeth, he said, "Get packed."

Katherine stuck her head around the corner. "Oh, good morning, Tony. Don't worry. We're all packed and ready to go. Arthur called us last night and told us to be ready to go home this morning. We've already had breakfast with those two, nice men from Interpol. And, not only that, they were kind enough to drive with us when we returned our rental car. So that's taken care of." She smiled at Tony with such an innocent smile on her face.

"And Arthur told us one other interesting thing. Did you know? He went to college with your Director's older brother? Isn't that interesting?"

The women walked to their packed suitcases standing at the end of their beds, pulled up the handles and began wheeling them to the door as if this were just another normal day of traveling abroad.

They had to stop, because Tony hadn't moved. He was still standing in the doorway. Every muscle in his body was as ridged as iron. His teeth remained clenched, his lips clamped shut. He was slowly taking in and breathing air out through his nose. He just stared at Katherine as she prated on gaily. If looks could kill, she would have been dead ten seconds ago.

Because the CIA plane wasn't a United States military plane it was able to land and take off at the Vienna International Airport. It was parked in a small hangar used for non-commercial planes. Tony and the women were driven to the hangar located south of the main terminal. When they arrived, Henri was waiting for them outside the building.

After Tony made the arrangements for the plane, he called Henri as a courtesy to let him know the CIA was flying the women home. He didn't mention his phone call from the DCI though. One could only take so much embarrassment.

After some chuckling from Henri, he told Tony since the arms deal had taken place on European soil, he wanted to travel with them to the United States to retrieve the diamonds himself. He added as diplomatically as he could that if he didn't fly with Tony and the women, once the CIA confiscated the diamonds in the United States, the legal red tape would make the return of them almost impossible.

The four entered the hangar through the office door. A gentleman from the Austrian Customs Department was sitting at a small table on the right side of the door. Each of them produced their passport. The man barely glanced at Tony's and Henri's before he stamped them. He examined the ladies passports more thoroughly, but finally gave them the necessary exit stamp.

Further ahead and on the left, a Marine guard was stationed at the door to the hangar itself. He was holding a metal wand. Katherine pulled on Pauline's sleeve to get her attention. With a very worried look on her face, she gave the barest of nods, more with her eyes than her head, toward the Marine and his wand.

Pauline understood immediately and had to fight down the panic. The diamonds! Oh, brother, she thought. The wand is going to light up and start beeping a mile a minute when it passes over all the diamonds in our boobs.

Tony walked over to the guard, removed his gun and belt and laid them on the table. He held his arms straight out and stood with his feet slightly apart while the Marine ran the wand over his body. No bells or whistles went off. When he was done, he picked up his gun, put it back in the holster, put his belt back on and proceeded through the door into the hangar. He turned and stood just inside waiting for the other three. Katherine was next in line. She approached the Marine slowly. Pauline was directly behind her and watched helplessly as Katherine seemed to shrivel up. Her shoulders slumped forward, her spine rounded as she desperately tried to pull her boobs into her body. The guard instructed Katherine to hold her arms higher. With her arms out and her spine still rounded, she looked like a whooping crane about to lift off. Here it goes, Pauline thought. Once the wand passes over her boobs, we're done. They're going to find out where we stashed the diamonds. They'll never allow us on the plane now. It's all over. For sure they'll make us fly home on a commercial plane all by ourselves. We'll be terrified all the way home. She wanted to weep.

The wand swept over the front of Katherine and nothing. Not a sound, not a beep, not a peep. Their heads popped up simultaneously. In that instant both of the women realized the wand was a *metal* detector. The diamonds must not be metal, so the wand didn't respond.

Pauline watched Katherine's spine unbend. Her posture became ramrod straight as the Marine finished up running the wand over her legs. He nodded to her when he was done. She took a few jaunty steps and sauntered through the door into the hangar area. When she turned around, she looked back at Pauline. She had her head held high, her shoulders back, and her boobs proudly thrust forward. Then she jiggled her boobs ever so slightly and gave Pauline a quick wink and a smirk.

Pauline had to look down at the floor to hide her smile. It wasn't because she was happy the wand didn't pick up the diamonds. She was stifling the smile, because of what Katherine looked like standing there. The saying *low handing fruit* flitted across her mind. Oh, my good friend, she thought. You have the ability to make life so much fun.

CHAPTER 41

The plane was small but seemed to have all the amenities. Along with the seats on the sides of the plane, there also was a conference area in the middle of one side. It consisted of a small round table and four comfortable chairs surrounding it. There was no flight attendant, so Tony went to the galley area and brought out coffee and boxes containing freshly made sandwiches, fruit and delicious looking pastries.

Once in the air, Henri and the two women chatted easily. When the women learned he was a grandfather, cell phones came out and pictures of the grandchildren were passed around. They also shared stories of the various countries of the world they had traveled to. Tony did not join in on the conversations. He remained quiet and just glared. The women seemed to intuitively understand he was still angry about how Arthur got the

Director of the Central Intelligence Agency involved in all this. They gave him his space.

Two hours later when they started over the Atlantic, Tony looked directly at Katherine and said, "All right, Katherine. Enough's enough. Tell us where the diamonds are."

The two women glanced at each other with a look as if to say, *the time has come.* They were safe and now they needed to keep their end of the bargain.

"Okay, Pauline, give them the diamonds," Katherine said with an innocent look on her face.

Pauline jerked in her seat. Her eyes narrowed. "You give him the diamonds," she snarled right back at Katherine. "Don't think I don't know what you're trying to do. You want me to make a complete fool of myself while you sit there like a princess all dignified and regal."

She looked over at Tony and said, "Give me your gun. I'm going to shoot her."

"I'm afraid I can't do that, Pauline, because I have first dibs on shooting her," was his reply.

"Hey," Katherine blurted out as she looked back and forth between the two of them.

After a moment, she sighed and looked across the table at the men. "All right, but you two have to turn around and face the other way."

"What the hell, Katherine? What does our turning around have to do with where you mailed the diamonds? Not a chance," Tony shot back. "If we turn our backs on you, I wouldn't put it passed you to try to jump out of the plane. I'll bet you two probably have mini-parachutes stuffed in your bras." The two women looked sideways at each other let out a stifled laugh.

Katherine shrugged and turned to Pauline. "Well, between us, we've had five kids, four operations and about, what - one hundred and fifty physicals? Everyone including the janitor has probably seen it all by now." She took off her sweater vest and laid it on the arm of her chair. "Your turn," she said to her friend.

Pauline sighed at the inevitable and removed her lightweight jacket. She took her time folding it before she too laid it on the arm of the chair.

"Are you sure you don't want to turn around?" Katherine asked the men one more time.

Tony just stared at them out of the corner of his eyes uncertain about what the women were up to.

As if on cue, the women began unbuttoning their blouses. Both men jerked back in their seats. There was a look of shock on their faces.

Pauline reached in her bra and brought out a hand full of diamonds. She dropped them on the small round table. Katherine did the same. The men watched in awe as handful after handful of diamonds came out of their bras. The pile on the table grew larger. The men had to hold their hands around the edge of the small table to contain all the diamonds.

When the women were done unloading their stash, they closed and buttoned their blouses. Pauline noticed how loose her blouse fit now. It no longer stretched across her boobs. She looked over at Katherine's boobs. Same thing. Her blouse seemed to drape. "Kind of disappointing, isn't it," she said to her friend. "We seem to have gone from looking like Dolly Parton to looking like Twiggy."

Katherine looked down at her chest. "Good grief. I'll be able to see my feet again when I stand up."

"Mon Dieu," Henri said with a big grin on his face.

"Holy Toledo! Are you telling me you two have been running around all this time with these diamonds stashed in your bras?" Tony asked. Gone was the anger. It was replaced with mirth. A smile formed. With lips pressed together, he began to laugh silently.

"We couldn't figure out where else to keep them," Katherine said. This caused Tony to laugh out loud.

"You're saying you had these in there," Tony said pointing to their chests, "The whole time you were in the warehouse yesterday morning?"

Both women nodded in agreement.

Tony looked over at Henri. "Geez, it looks like there's over a million dollars in diamonds," he said chuckled.

"That's what we figure too," Pauline said. "I know this seems funny to you, but in truth, it's been so scary."

"It is over," Henri responded immediately. The women had to understand they were safe. They had been through too much. "It is all over now, Pauline. Borovsky will stay in jail for the rest of his life. He has lost touch with reality and his network has already begun to crumble. All the threats he made yesterday are just empty threats now."

"Even so, it'll be a while before I can sleep soundly," Pauline said.

"I understand," Henri said and nodded his head.

When the plane touched down in Washington, D.C. and was taxiing to the hangar, Katherine looked over at the two men. "I want to thank the two of you for everything you've done," she said earnestly.

"I second that," Pauline said. "We really can't thank you enough."

"I know you think we were a lot of trouble, Tony," Katherine added. "But, things did work out. You caught Borovsky and now you have the diamonds back." She looked out the window. "And we got home safely. Thank you for that."

Tony nodded and tried to hide his embarrassment. "I'm glad you're home and safe too." He looked over at the two women and smiled. "And, I have to say, this case has certainly been an adventure. I don't know if there will ever be another one like it at the CIA."

"You know," Katherine added. "Think of it this way. How many other agents in the CIA are known personally by their Director."

Her comment wiped the smile right off Tony's face. "Don't push it, Katherine."

Katherine snapped her fingers and like a cartoon character, you could almost see the light bulb turn on in her head. "That reminds me. When I get home, I really need to send a thank you note to your Director for helping us." Tony slumped back in his chair. "Oh, don't worry, Tony. I'll be sure to mention what a good job you did catching Borovsky and how you helped keep us safe."

Tony leaned forward with his elbows on his thighs and buried his face in his hands. God help me. When the Director gets her *Thank You* note, my next assignment will probably be on some South Pacific Island inhabited by penguins.

Henri silently bowed his head and made an internal sign of the cross thankful Katherine didn't know the name of the Director of Interpol.

CHAPTER 42

The women's five children stood waiting for their mothers' plane to touch down. They were in a small hangar north of the main terminal at Reagan International Airport in Washington, D.C. Four of them were chatting and smiling freely. One was not. Dennis Maddich kept to himself off to one side.

"I think this adventure our mothers have been on tops all the other stunts those two have pulled. Can you imagine being mistaken for arms dealers?" Priscilla said laughingly.

Bernie joined in the laughter. "I'll have to agree with you, Pris," he said. "Remember the time they decided to take a walk in Yellowstone National Park and came face to face with the buffalo? When they turned around and slowly started down the path, it slowly followed them all the way back to the parking lot? I still remember the look on their faces when they came out of the bushes with this huge beast ambling along behind them."

"Oh, that's right," Pauline's daughter, Rosie chimed in. "I forgot all about that one."

"How about the Fourth of July picnic when those two decided to have fireworks in our backyard?" Jane asked. "Shooting them off caused the brush fire in the field behind us. Remember us kids running with buckets of water trying to put the fire out? Didn't the Fire Department issue Mom and Pauline a citation? And then they had to go to court." All but Dennis joined in the guffaws.

"Oh, you all think it was so funny," Dennis growled in the background. "We were just kids back then. We could've been seriously burned running around in the field. Our mothers have been nothing but trouble for years. And, there's nothing funny about this European stunt either." His lip curled as he looked at the four of them in disgust.

"Hey, come on, Dennis. Lighten up," Bernie said. "How many people do you know whose mothers were flown home in a CIA plane?" he added. He was trying to defuse the tension.

"Oh, sure this is all just one big joke to you. Well, I don't find any part of it funny at all," Dennis shot back.

"What happened to you, Dennis?" Jane asked. "You used to be so much fun when we were kids. You made me laugh all the time."

"I grew up," he said.

"Shut up, Dennis," Rosie said. She glared at her brother. "I am sick of listening to your repressive comments all the time. So just shut up. Your negativity drove your wife away. And now it's driving your kids away too." She nodded for emphasis. "Yeah, that's right, Dennis. The kids told me they don't want to visit you anymore. They're tired of you sapping all the joy out of their lives."

Her words seemed to give him a shocking wake-up call. This was his little mousey sister who never raised her voice. He couldn't even come back with a retort. He turned and walked to the far wall.

Rosie wasn't finished with her brother. "And, I'll tell you another thing," she said. "If you can't be happy our mother is coming home and is safe, then you leave right now, Dennis. Leave and go back to that lonely apartment of yours, because it's where you belong. I'm telling you if you say anything negative to Mom when she gets here after all she's been through, I'll never speak to you again. That's a promise." She did not back down, but continued to stare at her brother. The room was very quiet. Katherine's kids were looking down at the floor in embarrassment. No one said a word.

Fortunately before anyone could say another word, a man in a military uniform opened the door to the waiting room and announced that their mothers' plane had just touched down. It would arrive in a few minutes.

The five of them watched through the waiting room window as the plane taxied directly into the small hangar. The door swung open and the hangar personnel wheeled the steps to the plane. One of the pilots helped secure the steps. Moments passed before anyone else appeared in the exit door. Finally, they saw their mothers at the top of the stairs. Two men stood directly behind them. Katherine and Pauline waved to their children and started down the steps. The men remained in the doorway of the plane.

When their mothers got to the bottom of the steps, they turned and waved to the men in the doorway. The men waved back a little less enthusiastically than the women.

On their way to the waiting room, Katherine turned to Pauline and wiggled her eyebrows. "So how many diamonds are still in your bra?"

"Oh, about one or two," Pauline answered with a sly grin. "They were wedged so far up into my boobs, it was like they got sucked into a vortex. Unloading our bras in front of Tony and Henri was bad enough. I would have lost all my dignity scrounging around trying to pry those few loose. How about you? How many couldn't you get out?"

"About the same as you," Katherine said. "High five, Pauline," Katherine said raising her arm for the fiver.

They grinned and giggled as they smacked hands.

"Did you see the high five those two women just gave each other?" Tony asked Henri from the top of the plane steps.

"I suppose they are happy to be home," Henri answered.

Tony snorted. "In your dreams, Henri. I think they just gave each other the high five to celebrate the fact they didn't give us all the diamonds."

Henri looked over at Tony. "If that is so, my friend, are you going to be the one to call them back and grope around in their bras to check for stray diamonds?"

"Not a chance of a snowball in hell," Tony whispered as he watched the women enter the waiting room.

"Another American idiom?" Henri asked.

"Yeah, another American idiom," Tony said.

"Good one. I'm going to have to remember it when I get back home. I could use a, what did you say, *a snowball in hell* on a few occasions."

Katherine wished her arms were three feet longer so she could hug all her children at one time. She was so glad to see them. Everyone was smiling, crying and talking at once.

After Pauline gave Rosie a huge hug and wiped away her daughter's tears, she looked over at her son. "Oh, come on, Dennis. Give me a hug. I need it."

He gave her the slightest of smiles and brought his mother into his arms. "I'm glad you're home, Mom," he whispered in her ear.

"Me too, kiddo" she said and gave him one more squeeze.

Through her tears, Rosie gave her brother the thumbs up and a big smile.

CHAPTER 43

So this is the end of my tale about how random events happening in two different locations can affect one another, even across continents.

It took a while, but little by little our mothers told us the entire story about their time in Europe. At least we think they did.

The things they went through and how close they came to losing their lives still shocks us. We're all hoping our mothers' need for adventure are finally over for good. But knowing them, it's wishful thinking on our parts. Just yesterday they mentioned they were thinking about taking a trip to South America. They want to stand on the southern most tip of South America in Terra del Fuego and look at the churning waters of the Scotia Sea. Then they want to stop off in Buenos Aires and take tango lessons. Oh, brother.

Just to let you know, upon her return, my mother did indeed move into a senior condo. It's the same complex where Pauline lives. She and Pauline are now sporting brand, new, diamond earrings. The diamonds are huge. After what they went through, we all agree. They deserve them.

The only odd thing that happened is Arthur sold his house, and he too moved into the same complex as my mother. Now every time we visit, it seems she and Arthur are always together. And when they are, they're either holding hands or sitting very, very close to one another.

I wonder if they're having sex . . . Oh, Yicky! I'm not going down that road. This is my mother we're talking about. However, when I sort of hinted about how she and Arthur seemed to be together all the time, she just smiled at me and said, "Use your imagination, Priscilla." I thought I would faint.

ACKNOWLEDGMENTS

To my friend, Joy Hemmer, a retired nurse, who suggested and explained the effects of being stung by a bee.

To the kind people at Koehn and Koehn Jewelers in West Bend, WI who explained what raw diamonds would look like.

To the members of the Washington County Writer's Club for your helpful critiques.

To one of my daughters (nameless) and her former high school friend (also nameless) who explained the effects of smoking pot and for suggesting the women should crave munchies.

To my daughter Patti and James P. Scott for designing the cover.

BIOGRAPHY

Jackie Granger is a retired certified public accountant and vice president in corporate tax of a large financial institution who now runs a public speaking business.

Her travels have taken her to twenty-one countries, nineteen of them after she turned fifty-four. She even volunteered with the US Peace Corps in the former Soviet republic of Latvia when she was fifty-four years old.

Having written her first book after retiring, she continues to show that aging doesn't mean life has to end. She speaks publicly on the topic, "What is normal aging?" based on what scientists and not the media have to say. She is dedicated to proving that senior citizens are still active, smart, and willing to try new things—and that, yes, you *can* teach an old dog new tricks!

CPSIA information can be obtained
at www.ICGtesting.com
Printed in the USA
LVOW10s1133070517
533594LV00001B/44/P